Time Wall

Time Wall

S. D. UNWIN

Copyright © 2025 by S. D. Unwin

All rights reserved.

ISBN-13: 979-8308473909

For Heather, Stephen, and Gareth

1
Joad

Winter, 2037

The US Department of Temporal Security has a seal that looks like an eagle swallowing a clock. It seems more inspired by Peter Pan's crocodile than by the grave mission confronted by its predecessor, the Time Management Agency. Whereas the TMA had been a team of brilliant minds assembled to comprehend a shocking new physics and prevent its abuse, an organization in which I'd played a senior role, the DTS represents an entirely different region of the intelligence bell curve. Still, I'd be the last person to deny that the TMA had utterly failed in its mission. Had it given us any real understanding of the physics of temporal relocation? Or prevented the abject chaos that time travel caused? No on both counts.

The argument for dissolving the TMA and replacing it with the new clock-devouring DTS had been a strong one to the nation's higher-ups. After all, there's little point in having a clandestine organization to deal with the new physics when time travel and all its nefarious abuses have become an open secret. So now, instead of the covert TMA, we have a highly visible law enforcement agency located prominently by the Washington DC mall. Gone are TMA's headquarters secluded in the semi-arid scrublands of eastern Washington state; the large, shiny building that is DTS HQ boldly overlooks the Smithsonian Museum Castle.

The receptionist smiles over her desk counter in apology for the wait, but I'd expected it. The little prick who's keeping me waiting had once been a member of my team. I'd given him his job in the TMA, and then promoted him more than once, not because he had a first-rate mind, but because he'd been full of energy and practical ideas, and he'd been keen to please. Now, his second-rate mind towers above most others in the DTS.

"Dr. Bevan, Dr. Green is ready for you."

I'm snapped from my memories and follow the receptionist to his office, preparing for the task of addressing Green with civility and respect. I have no idea why I've been summoned this time. On the previous occasion, he had flown me out to ask a banal question he could have answered for himself with a web search, so I brace myself to be irritated and to conceal it. But alongside the incipient irritation is embarrassment. Does Green bring me to DC just to give me a sense of purpose... of worth? What's unbearable is the thought that Athol Green's motivation is actually pity.

And there's the supercilious grin. Green rises from behind his oversized cherrywood desk and offers me his hand. "Good to see you, Joad." As always, the man is well turned out, this time in an expensive dark blue suit, a crisply pressed white shirt, and a bright red tie. Back in the day, if someone had shown up for work at TMA dressed like this, they would have been abused savagely, perhaps even demoted on principle. He seems to have put on a few pounds since my last visit, and his thin thatch of yellow hair is becoming sparser. Scanning the highly polished recessed shelves, I see that he has accumulated more awards, and I glance out the large plate-glass window at an unimpeded view of the Smithsonian Museum. This is what success looks like in the DTS.

Green points at the chesterfield couch and I sit. "You're looking very healthy," he says.

I affect a smile. "You too, Athol."

"And what's new in the great state of Iowa? Job going well?"

"No complaints." The smile is becoming harder to maintain.

Green stares, expecting me to say more. "Look, Joad, I really wanted to set aside a good block of time to chat with you, but things just show up on my calendar." He points up, presumably to the floor occupied by the Secretary of Temporal Security. "It seems I'm supposed to be in a meeting right now. You remember what that's like."

I nod. "I do."

Green smiles at me. "But what's important is that I give you some good news." Before he can continue, there's a knock on his door and his assistant pops her head in. "Yes, yes, I know," he says. "Tell them I'm on my way." He turns back to me, that same placid smile on his face. "Joad, we're dissolving the Temporal Strategy Advisory Committee, so you're completely off the hook."

I wish I'd thought to affect my nonchalant smile an instant sooner.

"No more getting dragged across the country to deal with us DTS dolts." He grins.

"Okay" is all I can think to say as I'm being fired. I could ask why they've decided to terminate an advisory body of which they are in desperate need, but I won't give Green that satisfaction. Besides, his answer would irritate me—at least, that's what it would be designed to do—but I'd long ago become resigned to the fact that DTS are apes touching the monolith, relentlessly oblivious to the magnitude of their challenge, and too ignorant to know they're ignorant. That's the main difference between DTS and TMA: our ignorance had been self-aware.

Green knows the advisory committee is my only remaining involvement in policing the temporal issue. My only engagement in matters to which I've dedicated my professional life and most of my waking thoughts. Now that last strand of connective tissue is being severed.

I nod at my protégé.

I walk down Independence Avenue in the direction of the metro station. The frigid wind that has removed all feeling from my cheeks is now blowing loose trash in my direction. It seems the malaise has finally reached DC. Until now, the capital city had put on a brave face, making sure services were maintained and that civility appeared to prevail. It had only been a matter of time. In a world where a capricious timeline shift could, in an instant, wipe out a lifetime's worth of experiences and achievements, vanish loved ones, or even de-exist your very self, maintaining any commitment to personal responsibility, career, and civil society turned out to be too overwhelming a challenge for many.

Whether there will be a metro train in commission and going in my direction is, at best, a fifty-fifty shot. I steel myself to fight for a cab or, failing that, to brave the weather and walk back to the hotel. Despite myself, my thoughts return to Athol Green. Can I really blame him, or anyone else, for wanting me gone? What had I really achieved? Timeline dynamics are still almost incomprehensible, and TMA, in the end, had done nothing to halt the imbeciles hell-bent on taking up time travel as a sport. The Allfours, and others who amused themselves by violating the *one-second-per-second* rule, had run circles around TMA. Gallie would have called bullshit on these dark thoughts and pointed to everything we had achieved… How much worse things could have been without us. I can hear her voice, see her exasperated expression trying to cope with the wretched Joad Bevan. I miss Gallie. She had been—is—most of me.

TIME WALL

Out of the corner of my eye I see a figure approaching. The thin, unshaven man is wearing a T-shirt and jeans despite the arctic weather and has a look of casual violence about him. It's clear he's weighing me up as prey, but then smirks and walks away. That had been a sound decision.

2
Joad

All I can find is a can of tuna, but I'm not really hungry, anyway. I collapse into the threadbare chair by the window, scanning for suspicious activity. Two cars have been stolen from my apartment block over the past month, and another theft was probably due. On the positive side, there hasn't been a noticeable timeline shift in a while. Yet, it's easy to be deluded into thinking things are getting inexplicably better and that the shifts are becoming less frequent. I know better. There's the statistical inevitability that quiet patches will occur, and not every shift is going to affect me or change my reality.

I used to think being a tusker was a gift. Being able to detect the shifts instead of simply becoming part of the transition, acquiring the memory that comes with the new timeline. Now I see that for the tusker—the elephant that never forgets—it's a curse to remember the pre-transitioned world. What simplicity and calm it would have brought to my life if I'd been unaware of the family I'd lost. Something, somewhere had happened that had set the timeline in a different direction. Maybe it was the doing of a playful time traveler, or maybe just a dumb mistake by someone trying to do the right thing. But whatever had happened, it had caused reality to transition to a timeline in which my wife and son simply did not exist, one in which they were replaced by the cavernous hollow inside me.

Gallie had never been, and so all things of which Gallie had been the cause, including our son, had also failed to be. And if my body were not cursed with the tusker chemistry, then all I'd have known was the new timeline—its past and its potential futures. I would never have remembered embracing Gallie, playing catch with Casy. They wouldn't be gone because I wouldn't have lost them. They would have never existed. And there are no photographs or videos of them. Just the memories of a cursed tusker.

I hate tears. They had never been in my nature before, but that's something else the timeline shift had brought with it. It's beginning to rain and I close my eyes, listening to the patter on the windowpanes. Those trips to DC take it out of me, although I won't have to worry about that anymore. I'm now no longer in the time business.

It's over, thank God. These lectures are excruciating. Would it kill one of the dozen students in my severely undersubscribed class to just nod occasionally and show recognition that they've understood something. Still, I should be pleased that I'm working at all, and I'm okay with where I landed: Megara State College, the fifth-most prestigious academic institution in southern Iowa. The problem with being a senior manager in an organization that has been assiduously concealed from public view is that you don't have much of a résumé to show for it. There had been some talk of my taking up a position with DTS, but no way could I bring myself to do that. So here I am, teaching physics to students who seem to be enrolled in my course only because the Golf Green Design class was full.

"Dr. Bevan." I'm startled from my thoughts and don't recognize the student standing in front of me.

"Yes?"

"This must be soul-destroying for you," she says in an accent that sounds British. I'd become quite accomplished in my previous job at placing English language accents, not only in geography but also in time—but now an entirely redundant skill. Nevertheless, I'd say northern British, and contemporary. She looks a little older than the other students in my class. Her dark shoulder-length hair offsets her ruddy complexion, framing her face in such a way that I barely notice her crooked white teeth. Her intense blue eyes are waiting for my response. The other students, as always, had been eager to evacuate the classroom at the first opportunity.

"Occasionally," I reply. "I haven't seen you before, have I? Are you enrolled?"

She shakes her head and proceeds to sit on the edge of my desk. This young woman is not wanting for self-confidence. "I know you're busy," she says with no hint of irony while placing a document in front of me, "but this is for you." She points at the document. "I'd like you to read it."

"There are no assignments due."

"I know."

"So—"

"It's a report describing a physical theory you won't be familiar with."

Oh no. I always seem to attract them—the people who barely comprehend introductory physics yet have a new theory of the universe they need to share: a theory that had not occurred to the greatest minds in the field. I look at her rather than at the document and see no hint of sheepishness or reticence. Only the penetrating stare of her blue eyes.

The cover sheet of the paper is entirely blank. No title and no author attribution. That's unusual because crank authors are generally quite proud to take credit for their groundbreaking work. Even to read it superficially would be an evening squandered. Luckily, it's usually possible to identify the nonsensical premise of a crank paper just by reading the first page, and more often than not by the opening paragraph. "Leave it with me…"

"Alfreda Bell," she says. She looks like she might be about to say something more, some kind of sales pitch, but then she begins to navigate the desks towards the door. Halfway, she turns back. "You said Einstein was first to have the idea that gravity can be understood as curved space. Not true. Bernhard Riemann had that idea in the preceding century, but he couldn't make it work." She smiles once more.

She's right. Rude little shit.

3
Joad

The musty damp of my apartment building fills my nostrils as I ascend the creaky stairs, still holding the crank paper I'd been given. *Oh hell. I don't need this right now.* There are shards of wood around my shattered door lock and kick prints below it. This inelegant entry had not been the work of a professional burglar. I put my ear to the door, and hearing nothing, gently open it to peer inside. The occupant is looking into a cloth sack, likely assessing his swag.

"Find anything good?" I ask. A gangly youth stands there clutching the bag of stolen goods tightly to his chest. His greasy red hair hangs in his acne-filled face as he tries to turn his look of shock into one of bravado, which only accentuates his rodentine features.

"Just get out of the way and you won't get hurt, old man. *Go on!*"

It's on occasions like these that I wonder just how old I look. Too old to deal with this little moron? In fifth century BCE Persia I dealt with a foul-tempered Immortal, in ninth century CE Norway I stood down an axe-wielding Viking, and in the twelfth century CE I got the better of a Mongol warrior who'd taken an irrational dislike to me. So, for this skinny youth, I'm hard-pressed to summon even a drop of adrenaline. Then I recognize the kid. "You live downstairs, don't you?"

His eyes are darting around wildly, his intent to make a run for it obvious, so I have a decision to make. I can beat the living crap out of him and take my stuff back, or I can just stand aside and get it all back at my leisure, negotiating with his mother rather than with him. I let him make his escape.

In my darkest moments I take blame for all that's happening, at least until the Gallie in my head gives me the shit I deserve. It had never been so starkly clear to me that people define themselves by their past, their achievements, their experiences, their relationships. And when all that can change, or be annihilated, in the instant of a seemingly random timeline shift, can anyone be vested in themselves? Even if you're lucky enough to lack the tusker biochemicals and stay oblivious to the old timeline, you still live with the knowledge that all you've worked for and accumulated in life may be lost at any moment. I suppose the glass-half-full people may live in the wild hope that a new timeline will deal them a better hand, but if there's ever the hint of such optimism, it is overwhelmed by the dread of uncertainty. So where is the motivation to build a good life in a reality that is so fragile?

I know, I know, Gallie. I'm a miserable, despondent prick and should be thinking about ways to fix the problem. But how can I even begin to do that? TMA is no more. And be honest, Gallie, even with the full resources of TMA at its peak, were we really making a difference? Weren't we putting a Band-Aid on a sword gash? I smile. I always smile when I'm talking to Gallie, maybe because I see her beautiful face, or maybe at my own idiocy. *You know, my love, it was fucking lazy of you to be unborn. Would it have been so much trouble?*

I should be checking to see what my young neighbor has stolen, but I'm unmotivated. The crank paper is lying on the floor, my burglar having knocked it from my hand as he made his dramatic escape. A distraction would be welcome, so I take it to the couch. What nonsense does this blank cover conceal? I could use a smile right now.

Still no names to be seen, not even on the inside page. The author or authors have an uncharacteristic modesty. I scan the first paragraph—usually enough to reach a confident conclusion. But then I keep reading. Then I turn the page. My eyes widen. I'm soon on the next page, and then the next. My heartbeat quickens as I finish the introductory section.

Who is she?

An hour later, after the breathless turning of pages, I lay the report on the coffee table. I pace for a while before reopening it at a random page to just confirm what I had seen. My hands are shaking a little as I turn to the last page, blank but for two sets of numbers that can only be latitude and longitude coordinates. It's a location.

4
Joad

It's a fine rain and the windshield wipers are squeaking against the glass. My brain is still burning from the sleepless flight to Britain as I peer through the mist, trying to make out my surroundings. This area is called the Lake District, which, unless the name is ironic, means there must be lakes close by, but visibility is too limited to see one. What I do see are ancient stone walls lining a road so narrow that an oncoming car would be a problem. Behind the walls are open fields, scattered farmhouses, the remains of a castle, and the foothills of what may be mountains, although the hanging mist obscures them. Maybe the lakes are beyond there.

This all has a dreamlike quality. Out of nowhere comes a paper that explains things I'd spent a career trying, and failing, to comprehend. Even the unsurpassed genius of Ram Prasad had screeched to a halt in an attempt to fully understand the dynamics of temporal mechanics and the mutation of timelines. None of it had made much sense at the deepest level, even to the smartest of us. Yet its consequences turned out to be horrendous and ongoing. Gallie and Casy simply vanishing in a timeline transition, and my story just one of millions. What we figured out for sure is that Einstein had gotten time badly wrong. Time is something much weirder and more brutal than anything the great man had conceived of.

I jam both feet on the brake. *Shit!* My rental car and the cow blocking the road had narrowly missed a life-altering event. The large black creature with a thick white belt around its belly glances at me indifferently before moving on, unhurried.

I try to remember anything I can about the young woman who had approached me. Of course, there was no Alfreda Bell signed up for my course, nor was such a person registered at the college. It's the penetrating blue eyes and crooked grin I remember. And I had dismissed her out of hand. Just another toady student trying to impress the professor in any way possible except for actually doing the coursework. Damn, I should have opened the document right there when she'd handed it to me. It would have taken only a glance to see… Could she have done this work alone? Surely not. There had to be a whole research team, didn't there? Maybe she had just been the delivery service. I'm more than half a century old and have worked in the tackychemistry and temporal physics business for all my career, yet I've never seen anything like the report I was handed a day ago. When a new theory is launched, there is usually a sequence of papers that build up to it, so we all see it coming. But not in this case. Here, a fully formed, revolutionary theory had just been dropped from the sky. I remember the excitement and incredulity I had felt when I first opened a paper by the great Prasad, the father of tackychemistry. This felt no different. I take a breath, check for more cows, and drive on.

It's twilight and my GPS is telling me I'm fast approaching the destination coordinates. But this can't be right—I'm in the middle of nowhere. No buildings or structures of any kind, just softly undulating fields that rise into verdant hills.

Then I see it, a glow in the distance.

I turn through a gap in the stone wall and hear the crunch of gravel as I enter the parking lot. Hanging above the door of the small building is a shingle with the words *The Merry Crab* in blackletter font below a painting of a crustacean with flailing claws and crossed eyestalks. I get out of my car and walk to the entrance.

I've come this far to visit a pub?

If this were a trip from my time travel days, I'd guess that I'd landed in the Tudor period. There are posts and beams of oak, leaded windows, and a wood fire crackling on a hearth. But this Tudor house contains well-stocked shelves of booze and a rank of beer tap handles along a shiny wooden bar. Filling the space is the hum of conversations from patrons standing at the bar or seated around tables.

The barman gives me a nod. "Evenin'. What you 'avin'?"

I pick a name from the line of beer taps. This can't be it. This is definitely a pub. "Are there any other buildings around here?" I ask the barkeep as he pulls down a pint jug from one of the hooks above the bar.

"Other buildings, you say? There's Scalmere Village down the valley."

"No, I mean like a facility or laboratory or something like that."

He smirks. "Oh, you mean the large 'adron collider out back."

I smile once I get the irony. "Okay."

I take a deep swig of my beer as I look around. It's good. Very good. I'll find somewhere to sleep tonight and re-engage with my mystery tomorrow, once my brain has surfaced from its sleep-deprived fog. Maybe Scalmere has a bed to offer, and if not, I'm exhausted enough to pass out in my car.

Then I hear a woman's voice behind me.

"I've put on the new keg. See if it needs burping."

I turn and Alfreda Bell does a double take. Then there's the crooked smile.

"Well, it's Dr. Joad Bevan. About bloody time."

5
Joad

It irritated me that Alfreda had insisted I get a good night's rest before launching into the report and the list of questions I had prepared, but it seemed she was not the sort to have a change of mind. As I descend the creaking stairs the next morning, I can see the vapor of my breath. My night at the Merry Crab had been the coldest of my life, my blanket having had the heat insulation properties of plastic wrap; but that hadn't stopped me from falling into a deep, dreamless sleep. The pub windows are iced over and the embers of last night's roaring fire are glowing feebly. So what now?

I call out but there seems to be no one here. I unlock the door and step outside to the distant lowing of cows, but not much else. A rolling mist covers the hilltops between which I finally see a wedge of the eponymous lake. There's no sign of movement on the surrounding country roads, and my rental car is alone in the lot. I'm about to go back indoors when a distant set of headlights appears on the horizon of the colorless morning landscape, wending its way up the slope. As it pulls into the parking lot, the front window lowers.

"Get in," Alfreda says.

As I'm thrown back into my seat, I realize that she is not one for dallying.

"Where are we going?"

"Patience, Joad," she replies, her intriguing dialect making the first syllable sound like *pear*. After traversing the globe without sleep, then being stuffed into a bedroom the dimensions and temperature of a refrigerator, that's not advice I'm willing to take.

"Did you write that report?"

She smiles. "Did it interest you?"

"Of course it interested me. That's why I'm sitting here in a cloud of my own breath." I wait for a response but it doesn't come. "It's incredible work. You know that, right?" Still no response. "It seems to answer a lot of questions we've all been struggling with."

"Fucking cows." She sounds the car horn.

"I have questions for you. Or for whoever wrote it."

She's looking in the rearview mirror, still seemingly irritated by the cows, so I decide to just sit back in my seat and watch the sun peek over the horizon, filling the valley ahead with bright light.

Scalmere is a village of thatch-roofed cottages with front yards bordered by coiffed hedges and garden gates beneath trellis arches threaded with vines. It's the sort of place Agatha Christie would have assumed was populated by villainous vicars and their cheating wives, spending their weekends murdering parishioners, or solving said murders. We stop outside a cottage that looks particularly fictional with flower boxes beneath its windows, thick ivy on its single-story wall, and floret baskets hanging over the front door.

Alfreda pushes open the unlocked door to the cottage and with a majestic sweep of the arm, invites me to enter. I'm clutching the report, as I have been doing for the past forty-eight hours. The morning sun is flooding the interior through leaded windows, creating dust-filled shafts of light that illuminate the two Queen Anne chairs, Georgian coffee table, blanket-covered couch, and high-tech wheelchair inside. Baroque music plays softly in the background, and there's an inviting smell of cooking pastries. The woman seated on the couch looks up at me. At first she seems familiar, but I'm not able to place the where or the when. She has the same intense blue eyes and smile as Alfreda, but her hair is white and thin, her sallow skin taut over high cheekbones.

"I hope my daughter has been polite and respectful," she says in a soft, feathery voice. She holds out a slender hand of bone and veins, which I shake gently.

Bell… Bell. If this woman is also a Bell, does that shake loose any memories? It seems not. "Polite, but not very informative," I say.

"Are you hungry, Dr. Bevan?"

Having only eaten a continent ago, I nod. She points her daughter toward the room from which I assume the blissful smell is emanating.

"I think you recognize me," she says. "Do you?" I stare at her for a moment. "Perhaps you don't. I'm Victoria Bell."

My eyes widen. "Yes."

She waits, as if testing me.

"Victoria Bell. TMA." This woman had worked at the TMA Risley site. As I recall, she had been a fairly junior-level scientist, and as I try to remember any projects she had been involved in, none come to mind.

"Don't worry, Dr. Bevan," she says with a forgiving smile. "I was never really on your radar. I'm quite surprised you remember me at all."

Alfreda reappears holding a coffee jug in one hand and a two-tier serving platter in the other. It's full of pastries, and I decide my questions can wait. Mouth full, I nod at the report lying on the ornate coffee table between us. "Were you the author of that?"

Victoria Bell swallows, which seems to cause her difficulty. "My daughter and I are the authors."

I look at Alfreda who is busy slicing a tart. My first thought is that TMA may have seriously underutilized Victoria Bell; yet she'd really shown no sign of such potential. Or maybe it's just that no one had noticed it, including me. That's too embarrassing to contemplate. Was the reason something as appalling as her not being brash and overconfident enough to fit the profile for advancement in the TMA?

"Can we talk about this?" I say, picking up the report. I don't wait for a reply before launching into the questions I had scribbled in the margins. We quickly go deep, and it doesn't take me long to realize that the Bells are the real thing. Their knowledge of tackychemistry is encyclopedic and their understanding profound—not a case of just knowing all the terms and phrases, which can pass as expertise for many, but a rare depth of comprehension. And all this knowledge is only a point of departure for what they've achieved. I soon find myself a little lost in the discussions, exhausting my ability to even fake it, and sense the tables have turned—that they are testing *my* knowledge. I'm being served slices of tart by geniuses. Between them, they had dealt effortlessly with my questions and conveyed insights that had rapidly altered my perspectives, giving me a deeper understanding of what they'd been able to do. It's often the sign of monumentally great ideas that once you understand them, it becomes unfathomable why no one had conceived of them earlier. They are intuitive and obvious. Except that they had not been a scant hour ago.

I turn to the final section of the report about the practical application of their theory—about a form of travel that is entirely alien to me. "And you've done this? You've… taken such a trip?"

Although Alfreda had done much of the talking, she waits for her mother to answer this question. "We have not," Victoria says.

"Then how do you know that this could be possible… what you'd experience? You lay it out as if there's certainty and it's already been done."

"The theory is how we know," Alfreda says. "The theory tells us."

"You're that confident? Based on theory alone?"

"That's right." Alfreda's expression seems to be one of incredulity. "Did Einstein have empirical data when he produced the theory of special relativity? No. He had confidence in the logic, the elegance of the physical principles. He knew it had to be so."

"That's more the exception than the rule, Alfreda," I say.

"Yes, Dr. Bevan. I see you have a firm grasp of the obvious."

I turn to Victoria who is smiling at me. Then she begins to cough, but waves away the glass of water her daughter offers.

"Who else is there? Who knows about any of this?"

"One person," Alfreda says. "Our engineer. You'll be introduced."

I shake my head. "You'll have to forgive me for being a little stunned. TMA was a quasi-military government enterprise, whereas what you seem to have here is literally a cottage industry. And why here? Why at this location?"

"It's where we're from," Alfreda says, implying the question is stupid. I'm now beginning to understand that Alfreda reacts to all questions as if they are stupid. Victoria's focus has drifted to the window.

"And what about security? Maintaining secrecy? We had tiers of safeguards—"

"Well," Alfreda replies, "I suppose we could emulate TMA's success at keeping secrets if we put the report highlights on an airplane banner and fly it around the globe a couple of times."

"Fair point." I pick up my coffee cup but it doesn't reach my mouth before I ask, "Why me? Why are you bringing me into this?"

"Because you're Joad Bevan," Victoria says, having snapped back into the moment.

"We've reached the point where the theory needs to be tested," Alfreda says. "We need to see what's out there. And according to my mother, you have more experience of living out the theories than anyone. Thinking on your feet and all that. Coming back intact—that's important. Is she right? 'Cause if that's wrong, you need to be on a plane back to Iowa, where the buffalo roam or whatever the fuck happens there."

Victoria hisses something at her daughter, the content obscured by dialect.

"And including the engineer, only four people know of this? What you've done... what you plan to do?"

"It's Scalmere's little secret," Alfreda says.

There's too much to process over a slice of tart and a coffee, and I'm still not ruling out the possibility that this is all a fevered dream being had in a squalid apartment in southern Iowa. As unlikely as that is, it would make a lot more sense than it being real. Victoria nods for her daughter to refill my coffee cup.

"I've got to ask... how did you even begin to walk down this path? It seems plucked from the blue."

"You know better than that," Alfreda says with a familiar condescension, one to which I'm becoming resigned. "No science is plucked from the blue. We were actually working on the tachyon wall problem. Didn't make much progress on it but it took us in a useful direction." She nods at the report. It's true that hundreds of physicists have tried to solve the wall problem, but it seems that only the Bells failed forward so spectacularly.

I walk over to the leaded window and raise the edge of the flowery curtain with my finger. "You know, don't you, that this will get complicated?" I say. "People-complicated."

"Will it?" Alfreda raises her eyebrows. "And what does that mean?"

"Do you have a neighbor who drives a gray SUV with tinted windows?" It's the one I'd noticed behind us as we'd entered the village. Alfreda joins me and peers at the vehicle parked across the lane.

"No."

"Then it may have already begun."

6
Alt-Joad

Winter, 2037

The sign above the door flashes the words *Level 1 Clearance*, which is the reminder that if you don't have it, then you'd better not be here. Gallie is the last to enter the meeting room, but for her two minions walking one step behind. She takes her place at the head of the table. It's a seat that the chief of staff would normally occupy, but the understanding for today is that Gallie will be the center of attention in this meeting, and as the target she should be highly visible. The table is an oblong oval and about twenty people are sitting around it, all watching the secretary of temporal security adjust her seat. Sitting around the wall are twice as many people again—lower-ranking delegates from each federal agency represented. I am among them. Against the far wall I catch Athol Green glowering at me before quickly averting his eyes. Nepotism, pure and simple, is how I got my job. At least that's Athol Green's view according to my sources. And he has a valid point. It's possible that the job of assistant secretary for temporal operations may not have come my way if my wife had not been the secretary, but she had assured me that the president himself had insisted on it, and the Senate agreed.

There are quite a few highly ribboned uniforms around the table. All branches of the Department of Defense are here, along with State, Energy, Homeland Security, the FBI, and several three-letter intelligence agencies. Many of these organizations had made a pitch to have the newly formed Department of Temporal Security placed under them, but the White House was having none of it. The DTS would be an executive department, reporting directly to the president's office. And thank God for that. The prospect of taking on the politics of an existing federal department while at the same time trying to deal with the leviathan of temporal crime had caused night terrors for Gallie.

I watch my wife. Her beauty has not diminished an iota since the day we met. The perversion of time travel has made her a quarter of a century older than me, yet she's the one full of energy, in control, with an intelligence that almost glows, while I've been a little clapped out ever since the TMA had been dissolved. It had all been very traumatic, but we knew it made sense. Time travel and its abusers had become an open secret, so what became needed was a federal department to take on that threat overtly. But, had Gallie not been nominated and confirmed as the secretary of the new department, I likely would not have touched DTS with a barge pole.

An expectant quiet descends over the room. The chief of staff, a short, rotund man, adjusts his position several times before beginning. "I think we've all been briefed on what we're doing here." As usual, his tie shows evidence of his last meal. This morning I'd guess jelly donuts for breakfast. He's bald on top and his wavy gray hair, seldom touched by a comb, hangs over his ears and collar. He has never uttered a word that I've found impressive or interesting, but is redeemed in my mind by the fact that he seems to have great respect for Gallie, notwithstanding the common suspicion he has of anyone who started out with the TMA. There are *Level 1 Classification* markings on the reports laid out before each place at the table, although no one reaches for their copy as that would imply they had not already digested it fully.

The chief nods at the man in Army green. He has four stars on each shoulder and a sizable medal ribbon by his lapel. The general clears his throat, waves a finger at someone, and the room darkens. The wall opposite Gallie illuminates and an image appears. "Reconnaissance imagery stamped February 3, Southern Urals, Zhirdikstan," the general says. The satellite imagery shows a collection of makeshift structures and tents, with enough resolution to see people getting on with their lives, sitting in groups, walking between structures, children playing soccer or running aimlessly. "This is a Salkar refugee camp of about seven hundred people. The event occurs in eight seconds."

I look at the timer in the corner of the image, then back at the camp. There is a collective intake of breath when the event occurs. The camp—and all the structures, people, and animals—vanishes. It's simply gone, leaving an open terrain. No sign of physical stressors, no dust thrown up, not even a flash of light. The camp has simply ceased to be part of the image, as if photoshopped out. My eyes meet Gallie's. Then the screen becomes a wall again and the lights come up. Chairs swivel, heads turn, and Gallie is the focus of attention.

She taps her finger on the table, deep in thought. "And the assumption is that this is an accel event?" she asks quietly.

"We can think of no other explanation, Madam Secretary," the general says.

"What do you think, Gallie?" asks the secretary of energy. Only old friends get to address Secretary Jane Galois by that name, and the energy secretary, an old colleague from our days at TMA, qualifies.

"It certainly looks like it," she replies.

"Hard to imagine what else it could be."

TIME WALL

The room is quiet for a moment with an apparent understanding that Gallie must be the next to speak.

"Have there been other similar events?" Gallie asks.

"No." The woman who answered is an Air Force general, no less decorated than her Army counterpart. "But there are another eight Salkar camps within Zhirdikstani territory that are possibly vulnerable. We estimate around ten thousand Salkars at risk. It's possible—"

The defense secretary does not wait for his subordinate to finish her point. "So the question is—"

"I know what the question is, Jonathan," Gallie says. Her voice is calm, indistinguishable from the one she uses to request oat milk in her coffee. "Why didn't we detect the accel?"

She is, of course, exactly correct. That is the question. The technology to track accels, from origin to destination, is established. No longer could an accel event be concealed, detection resolution being so advanced that the individual tachyons that inevitably escape the most robust shield can be pinpointed. And this event had occurred in the wide outdoors, where shielding is the least feasible. If these were indeed accel events, then that would be a serious black eye for the DTS.

My stomach sinks as I have a flashback to the days when TMA was under fire from every punk federal department and member of Congress for failing to do our job. Is this how it all begins again?

"Yes, that is the question, Dr. Galois," the defense secretary says, probably believing his reproachful demeanor will unnerve Gallie. "If we can see the photons, why can't you see the tachyons?"

Gallie's unblinking stare is so long that even I begin to squirm. She finally turns to the Air Force general. "Do you think the Zhirdikstanis are weaponizing tackychemistry?" The defense secretary looks more nonplussed than irritated at being ignored.

The general casts an uncomfortable glance at her boss. "There's no technology that the Zhirdikstanis won't try to weaponize, Madam Secretary. We have always categorized tackychemistry as a dual-use technology, so yes, we believe that's what's happening."

"I'm sure the bastards would argue that this isn't about weaponization," the chief says. "That it's about humanitarian relocation."

"Can't we do a search for the victims?" asks a heavily bespectacled, skinny young guy in a dark suit and bright yellow tie. He's from one of the intelligence agencies. "We could rescue them, no?"

"No," the energy secretary says, interjecting a question meant for Gallie. "With the entire globe and the expanse of time to search, it's the proverbial needle in a haystack. More like a quark in a haystack."

"Tommy's correct," Gallie says. "It'd be impractical."

"The report agrees with your conclusion, sir," the Army general says to the chief. "This could be the leading edge of a systematic annihilation of the Salkars from the contemporary globe, sending them to God knows where. But wherever it is, we're guessing it's not a garden spot."

"And timeline implications?" the defense secretary asks. "With that many people being catapulted back, aren't timelines going to get screwed up? Won't there be a tsunami of shifts?"

Did Gallie just nod at me? *Shit.* "Joad?"

Why would she do that? This is not the sort of environment in which I perform well. I'm way too apt to deliver an uncontrollably frank assessment of things: circumstances and people. But all eyes are on me, so I clear my throat, casting Gallie a glance that only she would recognize as a threat of what's to come.

"We've done a lot of work on this," I say. "There seems to be a rule that the longer ago a timeline is perturbed, the less likely it is we'll see a detectable shift in the now. Inherent in the nature of things"—and I immediately regret using this term because at TMA it essentially meant I have no clue why what I'm about to say is true—"is a long-term convergence of timelines. If, for example, the victims were acceled back millennia, we'd likely detect no shifts today."

"Thank you, Joad," Gallie says, and Athol Green glares at me. If he wants to go places, he really needs to work on concealing his contempt.

"Was there any sign of a tachyon source?" the man from the intelligence agency asks. "Fixed position system? Ground vehicle? Airborne?"

"A low-altitude aircraft is all we could see, but it wasn't a tachyon source. It was probably just monitoring the camp," the Army general replies. "A subsurface system is a possibility, but unlikely. Synthetic-aperture radar is showing no signs of underground activity."

The chief of staff rests his hands on the rotund belly before him. "I want to go back to an earlier question. Is there no explanation other than an accel event? Are we one hundred percent sure?"

"We assessed some possibilities," the Army general says, pointing at the report, "but we could identify no other phenomenon that would result in instant loss of optical contact like that. It could, in principle, be done by data interference of course, but these are our satellites, our quantum-encrypted data streams, our analysis, and our visualizations. We're confident in ruling out fake data. The only—"

"Look," the chief barks, slapping his palms on the table, "what I'm not going to do is go back to my boss and tell him the Zhirdikstanis have tachyon-shielding technology that's a hell of a lot better than ours. Not unless we're one hundred percent sure." He turns to Gallie. "Dr. Galois, you need to prepare a report on possible explanations of what we're seeing, and what the hell we should do about it."

The Army general stirs, as if about to protest, probably because he thinks that his report has already wrapped up that matter, but the chief raises a finger at him. "DTS were not involved in the preparation of your report—a report that puts them in the crosshairs. I want to know what they have to say."

The general nods, sitting back in his seat. The chief is a good ally to have, but Gallie will know damn well that unless we can produce something quick and useful, that relationship will turn on a dime.

7
Alt-Joad

I wait in the limo for Gallie. *Shit. What a mess.* The driver opens the door and Gallie gets in beside me.

"Shit," she says, then taps the back of the driver's seat. "I've registered an accel."

"Risley?"

"Yep."

Although the TMA is now defunct, its original facilities in eastern Washington state are still a going concern, fully staffed and funded by the DTS. It's our jewel in the west where we keep all our monitoring, temporal acceleration, and experimental facilities, along with, in my own valid opinion, our best minds.

"Do you really think—"

"Is there another explanation?"

"None I can come up with."

The trip from the White House to the DTS is a short one, but longer than it used to be. Now there's the need to navigate street trash, bands of disgruntled citizens, drivers who don't see much point in following the rules of the road, and an ever-increasing number of security barriers.

"I can't think here," I say. "This is the wrong Washington for thinking."

Gallie's smile always takes me back to the first day we met. She puts her hand on mine. "I know what you mean," she says with the gentle southern drawl that's never gone away. "You can start thinking soon. But make it good."

One Washington is replaced by another as Gallie's office vanishes to be replaced by the accel monitoring hall in Risley. We could have acceled directly into the meeting room, but I always like to see my old stomping ground, as does Gallie if she'd own up to any sense of nostalgia. My wife and boss refuses to live in the past, which I tease her is quite a constraint given the profession she has chosen. I breathe in the air.

The sweet smell of tachyons. In fact, it's the smell of stale coffee and whiteboard markers. I follow Gallie into the meeting room. The director of research stands and shakes our hands, and I check that the *Level 1 Clearance* sign is illuminated as I close the door behind me. Victoria Bell, 'Ria' to most of us, has the bearing of an athlete: broad shoulders, narrow waist, and a lean frame. Beneath a shock of short brown hair, which could have been cut by her own hand using kitchen scissors and a small hand mirror, her high cheekbones and intense blue eyes give her a formidable air.

Seated at the conference table is Jeremy Chatham, a short, angular man with protruding ears, gibbous eyes, and a perpetual smirk. Not much younger than me, he was a veteran TMA employee before joining DTS, but had reached his full career potential long ago. Not a creator, not an innovator, but a solid calculator. Give him a miserably complicated set of calcs to perform and you can rely on him to do them quickly and accurately. And that's what he's been doing for decades under a string of bosses, all increasingly junior to him in years.

Gallie heads off the risk of time-wasting small talk by asking Ria to bring up the video file she had been sent. Ria nods at Chatham, and the video we had seen an hour before plays on the wall screen. Ria falls into a chair at the conference table and we watch her think.

"You told me what t'expect," she says, "but when you actually see it…" After all these years, my ear is fully acclimatized to Ria's vigorously retained north-of-England accent, and I know to take *t'expect* as two words.

"Jeremy, do me a favor," Gallie says. "Look one more time at the tachyon-monitoring dataset for that spacetime stamp." He taps his keyboard, displaying tables and graphs on the screen. We stare at them.

"Nothing," I say.

Gallie shakes her head, staring at Ria. "It's clean. Zero tachyon signature." This is how my wife puts the pressure on a director of research who might be thinking that we're all in this together. Gallie can be a little ruthless that way, although these two women have a relationship that I can't claim to fully understand.

Ria had been Gallie's discovery, her protégée. That's one of Gallie's many talents—recognizing a diamond in the rough. But I flatter myself that I also played a role in Ria's education as a temporal scientist, having tutored a painfully straight-laced physicist on the importance of a sense of humor, or at least an appreciation of the ludicrous, which in our business is crucial. If maintaining sanity is a career objective.

Ria looks at me and I flash a smile intended to be a comfort ahead of the likely oncoming interrogation. "Okay," Ria says, rubbing her forehead. "And you think…It's the only possibility… Is it? Yes, what else could it be?" We don't interrupt Ria's soliloquy.

Events of the last few months have been unnerving. It started out with an experimental anomaly during a routine operation to accel an electronic unit up the timeline. The device had winked out, as expected, but something strange then occurred. There had been no collateral tachyon flux detected. In any accel event, the local tachyon field should peak, but on this occasion, it had not. Worse still, the device could not be tracked along its intended accel trajectory. It just vanished. We'd all had the same horrifying thought.

What if that accel had involved an operative? That scenario was too awful to contemplate.

Equipment was checked, backup-monitoring data were scoured, but nothing showed up. There had simply been no tachyon event. All accels were then immediately put on hold and we launched a full-scale incident investigation. And the finding? We'd apparently been supplied with the incorrect isomer of Chemical 1 of the three tackychemicals, which, when mixed, produce a tachyon transportation flux. Simple as that. The tackychemistry had been screwed up.

Until then, I had always assumed that either the particular chemical isomer used in the reaction did not matter to tachyon production, or that if you used the wrong one, there would be no reaction at all. So much for assumptions.

So now we have dots that we're forced to connect. A refugee camp and the hundreds of people who lived in it popped out of existence, with no sign of a tachyon flux. None.

I say what has, as yet, been unsaid. "An *effon* event?"

We had been working on the assumption that if it wasn't tachyons entraining and transporting the vanishing matter, then it must have been some other particle. A *WhatTheEffon* was the working name we'd given it, but without a theory or model, there was no way to develop a detection technology. So that's the bus under which we're now throwing our director of research. It should be a great compliment to her that we consider hers one of the finest minds in the DTS, but I'm guessing that right now she's not feeling it. Ria has the air of a coyote looking up at a falling anvil.

"Where are we on detection, Ria?" Gallie asks.

"I wish I could give you better news, Gallie, but—"

"Okay," Gallie says.

"We're going deep into Prasad's tackychemistry and temporal physics models, as well as all subsequent developments, just to see if we should have any expectation of symmetries, of a second particle. But we're drawing a blank. Prasad's work points to tachyons and to tachyons alone."

"Can we even assume that these effons are sending matter up and down the timeline?" I ask, hoping to give Ria an opportunity to share a morsel of progress.

She shakes her head. "Not really. If they are, we can't track them. Where else they could be relocating matter to, I don't know. And it's possible, I suppose, that it isn't being relocated anywhere, and that the matter is simply being annihilated."

Gallie grabs at her hip, and I tell her to sit down, but she dismisses the suggestion with a shake of her head. I pull out a chair from the conference table, intent on getting my way. My wife's mind is still as sharp as a tack, but despite being in her eighth decade of life, she outright rejects the idea that her body has not kept up. She sits down, aggravated at my persistence.

Chatham is still mesmerized by the screen of data, and Ria places a hand on his shoulder. "Thank you, Jeremy, we'll let you get back to your day." Ria waits for him to leave before asking, "They still don't know? The DC higher-ups?"

Gallie shakes her head. "No one but us and your team knows, Ria, and we'll keep it that way until we understand enough to make a useful recommendation. All we need... all the world needs right now is a little more chaos that we can't do anything about." Gallie looks directly at Ria. "Is your team safe?"

"Of course it is," she replies. Gallie lets the silence hang for a moment.

"What the White House does know is that the Zhirdikstanis have a weapon that vanishes people en masse."

"If it is effons, might they have an understanding, the Zhirdikstanis? A background theory?"

"We don't know," Gallie replies. "To do what they're doing, they wouldn't need to know any more than we do. They could have discovered the effect of the altered isomer by accident, just like we did. And being Zhirdikstanis, *weapon* was their first thought."

I slap the tabletop. "Okay, here's the deal. Gallie and I are going to stay here for a while. The fuse is short and we'd better come up with a few answers very quickly." Ria is too late to conceal her grimace. "I know, I know, but we won't get under your feet. We'll just provide the input and resources you need. And that's it. The truth is, being away from DC will do us both good—give us space to think." I look at Gallie, bracing for the pushback, but she nods.

"Joad's full of shit." Gallie has a wry smile. "Of course we'll get under your feet, but as long as we're here, those higher-ups can't get under *our* feet. We'll stay in the apartments." Gallie rubs her hip again. "So let's sketch out a plan for the next forty-eight hours."

8
Joad

A healthy paranoia is what has kept me alive for this long, and I'm still hoping I'd been wrong about being tailed by the gray SUV. Here I am, lecturing the Bells about security, and now it seems I may have been the one to bring trouble to their doorstep.

But who could it be? Who'd be tracking me, thinking I'm involved in something of interest to them? With a mind still fogged by jet lag, I don't have the bandwidth to take on this challenge right now. I do miss the days of the accelerator. A blink of the eye and I'd be where and when I needed to be. The momentary disorientation after an accelerator jump is infinitely better than the extended jet lag that only gets worse with age. If I'd had a little gumption, and not been such a prissy rule follower, I would have kept an accelerator for myself—something in the closet for emergencies.

It's evening and the Merry Crab is buzzing. The tables are full tonight and a crackling fire is keeping out the bitter chill of a Lake District winter. As the American, I'm getting a lot of attention and seem to have been pulled into the drinks rounds system, guaranteeing that tomorrow morning will be full of regrets. It's difficult to penetrate the local accent, but smiling and nodding is generally the right response. Now and then I get a furrowed brow, maybe I'd smiled and nodded at the wrong thing, but the awkwardness always passes quickly, carried in the stream of warm beer.

Alfreda the publican is busy behind the bar and paying me little attention. I make a mental note to ask her how this had become her second job. And she's good at it, knowing all the locals by name and their favorite tipples. I'd assumed that Alfreda, like her mother, had been with TMA, but I'd been put right about that. After getting her doctorate, it seems she had been entirely home-schooled in tackychemistry. And quite a job her mother had done. How the hell had we missed this woman at TMA? Other than Prasad himself, it now seems she'd had the finest mind in the entire organization. And that had gone unnoticed? Shame on us, on me.

I take a swig of my beer, glancing along the bar at a woman smiling at me. I look behind me to make sure I'm the intended recipient of the smile and then smile back. Her pixie-cut is gray but for a turquoise tint, and she has deep smile lines with kind eyes. She moves up to the bar stool next to mine.

"You're fresh meat, I'm afraid," she says. "That gets you a lot of attention."

With my inhibitions long gone, this is enough to start up a conversation. It seems her sister is the Scalmere local and she visits her from London a few times a year. She has kids in college, and mentions in a matter-of-fact way that she's lost friends to timeline shifts. As a tusker, she shows the kind of emotional detachment from timeline snaps that preserves sanity, if you're able to pull it off. I suppose it depends on the magnitude of what you've lost. I'm miserably drunk at this point, and this feels like the first real conversation I've had with another human in a long time.

She follows me up the creaking stairs. Once we're behind the closed door, we kiss, and a wave of angst beginning in my stomach slowly envelops me. What would Gallie think? I don't have to guess for long because her familiar voice enters my head, and this time her tone is waggish.

Man up, Joad. I've been gone for six years, so don't be such a damn wuss. It's okay to be happy now and again. Just set realistic expectations—she won't be in my league.

I smile as I lead my new friend to the small bed.

The first time I awoke in the night she was still there, my arm across her stomach, rising and falling as she breathed gently. But this time she's gone. Embarrassment washes over me as I realize I hadn't even asked her name. Am I suddenly *that* guy? No, I need to give myself a break before Gallie shows up.

I lie on my back feeling clear-headed, my respite from thinking about the report now over. As much as it explained, it created its own questions. I think back to the shock I had felt early in my career when I learned that a simple chemical reaction could produce a firework of tachyons, the faster-than-light particles that entrain matter and fling it up and down the timeline. Like every other physicist in the know, I'd experienced a mix of indignance and amusement that it's mere chemistry that enables time travel, not some high-energy physics setup. It's the simple reaction of three chemicals, discovered entirely by accident, and it took the genius of Ram Prasad to explain it and figure out how to manage it—how to control time travel.

But then came the stark and brutal reality of timeline transitions that were the consequence of this new physics: Actions that could divert us to an entirely different timeline, with its own well-defined past and future, meant that not every one us would survive that transition. Because some timelines have no place for us. And discovering the rare phenomenon of being a tusker, someone who retains the memory of the old timeline, revealed that everyone else's memory of the old timeline is entirely supplanted by a memory consistent with the new one, making them oblivious to the transition. What had become instantly clear was that anything we had thought we understood about time had been wrong. And after the greatest minds had failed to understand any of this, out of the blue descend the Bells.

I sit up, draining the remaining drops from my bedside water glass. I really need more fluid than that to avoid a miserable morning, but it's too damn cold to venture out to the bathroom.

What Victoria and Alfreda had done was to realize that tachyons weren't the loners we had assumed, but in fact had a partner. They had named this new particle a *koson*. And what they'd proved is that while tachyons can sweep objects up and down the timeline, kosons can carry objects *between* timelines. This is a mind-boggler, at least in my limited frame of reference. They go sideways—perpendicular to tachyons. And, most unfathomable of all, this means we can, in principle, transport ourselves between timelines… at will.

Until now, all our conventional wisdom told us that reality and life are defined by a single timeline, the others existing as no more than ghostly potentialities, waiting to have the fire of reality breathed into them. But now… My excitement transitions to nausea and I take controlled, deep breaths.

And the Bells think they have the technology to do it—to take a trip with the kosons, to traverse timelines. But what the hell does that even mean? What exactly do they think they can do? The technology to do it is as simple as using a different isomer of one of the three tackychemicals. That's enough to produce kosons instead of tachyons. It's that damn simple. I lie flat, still trying to control my breathing.

TIME WALL

And they want me, Joad Bevan the adventurer, to try all of this out and take the trip. I pull the blanket up to my neck, roll onto my side, and curl into a fetal position. As I drift back into sleep, my thoughts are of timelines that contain the things I want, the things I love.

9
Joad

It's another frigid morning as I descend the creaking stairs to make coffee. There's something about standing behind a pub bar that gives a sense of authority and power, compared even to being the director of several hundred time travelers. I scan the shelves under the bar for filters and coffee.

When the door bursts open, Alfreda enters on a wave of icy air and rain. She leans against the door, closing it against the cold wind. "The SUV was there all night," she says. "Is my mother going to be safe?"

"It's probably nothing. And if it is something, it's likely just surveillance of me." Maybe I'm flattering myself, but I will get to the bottom of it—I still have contacts. "It didn't follow you here?"

"I don't think so." She takes off her scarf and anorak. "So have you thought about it? Are you on board?"

"Yes, I've thought about it, but what I need to know is what exactly the plan is, Alfreda."

"Okay, so first, I'm Alfie, not Alfreda." She crosses to the bar and checks on the brewing coffee. "The plan is, we take a trip. We fly with the kosons, cross timelines."

"And do you have any sense of what that actually means? Crossing timelines? That isn't a term that has conventionally made sense, is it?"

"I know, I know," she says. "It's not intuitive, but what the hell in temporal science *is*? The model has it laid out just fine. The physics is unambiguous."

I shake my head. No matter how pristine the mathematics, the visceral, human experience of it is another matter—entirely unpredictable. The math says nothing about that.

"Okay, then," I say. "So we all know that 'reality' transitions between timelines continually—it's a nasty little gift from the new physics and time travel—but what we're talking about here is actual individuals, humans, propelling themselves between timelines. That's easy to say, but what the hell does it mean? And don't tell me about the equations. I'm not asking about the math."

"Well, that's what we find out, isn't it? That's what we're going to do. You want the answer first? That makes no fucking sense."

She's right, but I need to play this out. Both of us know damn well that I'm going to proceed with this crazy project, but affecting some hesitation is important to my sense of reason and dignity, until the conversation inevitably slides into theory. It's a comfort zone for us both. Talk of particle symmetry groups, renormalizability of field theories, and Feynman diagrams is a lot less unsettling than the real prospect that physics will throw us a curve ball that rips us out of the very fabric of reality. I may be too conservative, but remaining part of reality doesn't seem like an unreasonable demand.

Alfie stops an arcane explanation of some technicality mid-sentence. "Look, are you with us?" I hesitate and she purses her lips. "Stop this fucking about, Joad Bevan. You've already decided and now you're just dicking us about. We can go it without you, no question, yet for some reason, my mother thinks your experience will help. Maybe it will, but I'm not going to let your dithering slow us down."

I smile. "Okay, Alfie. Okay, I'm in. But if it doesn't cause too much inconvenience, I'd like to ask more questions that might lower the odds of us annihilating ourselves. Is that okay with you?"

"No need for sarcasm," she says with a smirk. "I'm not entirely on board with annihilating ourselves either."

"Good." I pick up the report from the bar. "We have a lot to discuss. But first, a trivial matter. Why the name 'koson'?"

"I was in Greece, fifth century BCE."

I'm taken by surprise. So there's more to her than theory. And she wasn't in TMA. That leaves very few legitimate reasons she might have been a time traveler, but that matter can wait.

"*Kos* is a word they used for a crab." She stares at me as if to see just how slow I am.

"Kosons travel sideways across timelines. Okay, setting the theories aside, where are your material resources? A stack of paper won't make your crab particles."

"Our engineer is on his way. There are stale donuts under the bar. Pass me one."

The door bursts open again followed by another arctic blast. The person stepping in is heavily bundled in a hooded parka, gloves, and scarf. He pushes the door closed and begins to peel off the layers, throwing them to the floor. When he notices me, he stares without tact. He has dark skin, short black hair, and a stubble beard, having more the appearance of a Bollywood leading man than an engineer.

"Mo Khara, meet Joad Bevan," Alfie says. Without acknowledging the introduction, he walks past us and descends the stairs to the cellar. Alfie gestures that I should follow. We navigate beer kegs, hoses, and cardboard boxes of pub snacks until we arrive at a closed door. It's secured by a loop, hasp, and padlock, and the Bollywood star feels around in his pocket.

"Your equipment is behind there?" I ask. Alfie nods and I can't help but smile. "At TMA, our critical assets were protected by multiple redundant security systems—physical, cyber, and temporal. And what you have here is a padlock."

"It's a pretty sturdy one," Alfie replies.

Mo Khara inserts his key, removes the padlock, and pushes the door open. He flicks on the lights and before us spans a low-ceilinged, windowless room of about thirty by thirty feet. There's a seemingly random array of cheap metal-framed Formica-surfaced lab benches, some covered with flasks, beakers, plastic tubing, burners, and bottled chemicals, others with micro-electronic components, soldering irons, oscilloscopes, and precision electronics tools. It all looks like something you might find in a high school.

"This is it," Alfie says.

"This is it," I echo.

"This is Mo's world," she says. "Something of a hands-on genius, our Mo. Well, at least when he's not being a moron." She smiles at her partner, but he's too busy glaring at me to notice. It's quite often that I don't hit it off with people, but at least I usually know why.

"I'm guessing you're ex-TMA," I say to him. He looks maybe a decade older than Alfie.

"I just want you to know," he says, "that the decision to bring you into this project was not unanimous." He has the same accent as Alfie.

"So now I know. Have we met before?"

"TMA was an abject failure," he continues. "It did nothing to secure the timeline, and even less in understanding temporal mechanics. A comprehensive dead loss. Why we'd want to take on a TMA manager, I don't know. So you can sprinkle your magic dust of success on us?"

I turn to Alfie, assuming the question is really for her.

"Mo," she says in a threatening whisper, "we've been through all this bullshit and you agreed." There's a brief standoff and then Khara musters a quick nod. The problem with being a senior manager in a big organization is that there will be people who hate you for reasons of which you're unaware. Sometimes you're even unaware of the people. *He can't be blaming me personally for TMA's failure, and so I'm guessing there must have been some stupid little thing I once did to piss him off. That's how it usually works.*

Brushing past me to one of the electronics benches, he picks up something that looks like a bulky wristwatch, with a dark, blank screen. Sullenly, he holds it up. "This is it… the final product." I raise my eyebrows. "It's our accelerator."

I squint at it. In the most refined and miniaturized accelerator I'd seen, it had been a device that straps onto the forearm, consisting of three chemical chambers, a reaction vessel, a micro-injector, and a controller. *This watch surely can't contain all of that.*

Khara is enjoying this moment of incredulity. "First improvement was increasing the efficiency of the chemical reaction that produces the tachyon blast. With our mixing technology, microquantities of the three chemicals are enough to create an adequate entrainment wave. Also, the controller that mixes the chemicals in required proportions and rates is molecular… nano-scale. This does everything a conventional accelerator can do, but with better efficiency and veracity. It can land you with an accuracy of four minutes in a century, an inch in five hundred miles."

I can't help but grin as I take the device from him, rolling it over in my hand. It's cold and heavy.

"And the good part…" Alfie says, prompting Khara to continue.

"There's a fourth microchamber in there. It contains a different isomer of one of the three chemicals. Use that variant isomer and what you get is a blast of kosons instead of tachyons."

"Which blasts you sideways across timelines?" I'm saying this as if I understand what I mean.

"That's the theory," he replies. In that answer, I sense a level of confidence that falls short of Alfie's unbridled certainty. "In fact, we can create reactions involving all four chemicals that can pinpoint a destination across and within timelines… we think."

"A tachyon/koson cocktail?" *Carrying the victim to God knows where.* The Bells had begun to build up in me a level of confidence in this boggling science, but now I feel myself backsliding. Maybe it was seeing the hardware—a miracle too far.

Who are these people, after all?

10
Alt-Joad

I leave Gallie to rest, my body too full of adrenaline and my mind too crammed with scenarios, risks, and consequences to sleep, so I take a car and make the short journey through the arid terrain of the DTS site, down the highway, and into the town of Risley. Having grown up here, I enjoy driving past the old haunts that are still standing. But things are seldom the same twice. Some change is because of the normal evolution of a town, some because Risley has not been immune to the global anarchy and violence, and some, most disturbingly, because of timeline mutations.

I think about the pressure we're putting on Ria. What we've asked for is unrealistic, absurd even. It had taken Ram Prasad the best part of a decade to develop a coherent theory of temporal physics, and now we're telling Ria and her team to come up with an understanding of effons in a stupidly compressed time frame. One difference between Gallie and me is that my inclination is to let Ria know we think our demands are ludicrous. But I guess that's why it's Gallie who's the secretary of the DTS. And there's no denying she usually pries superhuman performance from her team, although, as *good cop*, I flatter myself that I sometimes have something to do with it.

Most places are closed at this hour so I just cruise down familiar streets, waiting for any hint that sleep is in my near future. I stop at a traffic light near the middle school track where I used to excel at the one hundred yards dash, at least until Donny Rose moved here from Seattle and broke my spirit. That little shit was fast.

A car pulls up beside me and I glance casually into its passenger-side window, doing a double take just as the car is pulling away. I sit for moment, unsure of what I had seen, then follow the car as I activate my phone.

"What time is it?" says a croaky voice.

"Sorry, Ria. Hey, is Athol Green visiting Risley right now?"

"What?" She clears her throat. "No, not that I know of. Why would he be?"

"Can you check with the access control officer?"

Ria is too tired to show curiosity. "I'll call you back."

I follow the car at a distance, and after a few minutes my phone rings. "No, Green isn't in Risley," Ria says. "And be warned, our access control officer wasn't overjoyed at being woken up at this hour."

"Yeah? Well, wait twenty minutes, then call him back to express my thanks."

We're beginning to ascend the Badger Mountain foothills in South Risley, heading towards a building estate. I turn off my lights and follow the car around the labyrinth of residential streets until it stops outside a house in a row of stucco homes. The driver is definitely Athol Green. I recognize the heroic gait as he walks up the path, arms angling out like a gunslinger about to draw two pistols. The door opens and warm light spills onto the path.

I get out of the car and walk up the slope towards the house, avoiding the direct spotlight of the street lamps. The front rooms of the house are in darkness, so I cross the side lawn to take a look into the back, running the last few paces to get behind a tree. I squint into the back room. One is Green, the other... Jeremy Chatham. That is beyond interesting. They seem to be exchanging words and then Chatham removes something from his pocket and hands it to Green.

I have options. I could barge in and demand answers. But Chatham is one of Ria's key staff and she seems to trust him. If there's an innocent explanation, the barging-in scenario would embarrass everyone, even damage a few relationships. But what the actual hell could an innocent explanation be for Green visiting a junior scientist in the middle of the night? And why didn't he just accel to Chatham's home if he wanted a face-to-face? Why drive there? If I wanted no record of having visited someone, I'd do the same. The second option is to wait until morning to question Chatham, but then he could easily deny handing over that small object. So now that I've gone through the specious exercise of weighing up my options, I'll proceed as I'd always meant to.

I slip back around to the front of the house and rap on the door. After a few moments, it opens. In Chatham's face I see the priming for rebuke give way instantly to shock. Sweeping past him into the main living room, I walk directly to Green.

"Ha. I *thought* it was you," I say. "I saw you downtown and just wanted to... say hello." Green's face is still. "Hope you don't mind." He hesitates and then shakes his head. I've always thought it a paradox that a battle of wits is one type of confrontation that can be lost because your opponent is unarmed, so I avoid that embarrassment. "What business brings you to Risley, Athol?"

"It's not related to the Operations Division," he says, unruffled.

"So, it's research-related. Jeremy is a key guy, but it's not really protocol to go directly to one of Ria's team, is it? She might not appreciate that."

"I don't want to ruffle any feathers, Joad. I'll talk to Ria tomorrow."

"Thank you." Jeremy Chatham is looking terror-struck and I smile at him warmly. "Oh, before I leave you to it, what was the thing Jeremy handed you?"

"What? Not sure what you're referring to." As he tightens his fist around the concealed object, he attempts to smile back at me but it comes out as an ugly grimace.

"Sure, he passed you—"

My head lurches forward as something sharp connects with the back of my skull, but before the pain can register, a black cloud explodes behind my eyes.

11
Joad

During the long discussion with Alfie and Khara on the tackyengineering of their accelerator watches I begin to feel that my comfort zone is now at least within telescopic sight. They do seem patient with me, and for that I give them credit. If it were me doing the explaining, I'd be shaking my head, sighing, and barking insults that revolve around their intelligence and that of all their forebears.

"What testing have you done?"

Khara lifts a coffee-stained document from a bench. "The test protocol, setups, and results are here."

"All tests so far with inanimate objects, of course," Alfie adds. "First one, we put a watch on a can of beer programmed for a round trip."

"And…"

"It returned. Intact and drinkable." She holds up an empty beer can. "In all tests, our sample got home safely."

"Okay, so let me ask you this. We know how to measure distances in space and time, and the strength of a tachyon blast needs to be about proportional to the distance you want to travel. But when you're moving between timelines—between realities—what's the equivalent of distance? How do you know how strong a koson blast you'll need?"

Khara and Alfie exchange a glance, which is not encouraging. "We assume," Alfie says, "that the more similar two timelines are to each other in terms of the realities they represent, the closer we can define them to be."

"That's your speculation?" I ask. Khara shrugs. A terrifying shrug. "Say your speculation is wrong. Say a weak koson blast doesn't take you to a similar reality but to one in which... there's nothing but the hard vacuum of space. What if you haven't got your arms around koson physics at all?"

"Look—" Khara begins, and Alfie raises her finger to shut him down.

"You're exactly right, Joad. We don't have that aspect of the theory totally nailed down. But look at the tests," she says, pointing at the coffee-stained document. "We've transported cameras, and the places they wind up look a hell of a lot like where they set out from. No vacuums of space. No dinosaurs or alien creatures, for that matter. Just a tiny lab in Scalmere."

"Need to piss," Khara says.

I wait for him to exit, now having the chance to ask a few questions meant only for Alfie, but as he reaches the door threshold, he flies backwards, landing hard on his rear. A bulky black man with a shiny head, sporting a dark-blue suit, strides in confidently. The man who follows him is tall and tanned, wearing a white shirt under a bomber jacket. He looks older but trim.

Alfie steps towards them. "Who the hell—"

"You stop exactly where you are," says the tall one. His accent is distinctly American, maybe Boston. He looks around the room and seems to be fighting a grin. "We have here a tackychemistry laboratory, don't we?"

I can tell from the hang of the bald guy's jacket that he's carrying a gun.

I smile. "DTS, I assume."

"Why would you assume that?"

"Oh," I reply, "it's just that I sensed the average IQ of the room plummet when you walked in."

The tall one smirks while the guy carrying the gun remains stony-faced.

"Dr. Joad Bevan. You of all people involved in something like this. Why wouldn't you know better?"

"You're a little outside your jurisdiction, aren't you?" I say.

"We work with our British partners," the tall one says, nodding towards his colleague.

"This isn't a tackychemistry lab," Alfie says, and the tall one can no longer conceal his grin.

"Well, we can see if that's true after we impound all of this. And we'll also need to find a comfortable place for you while we confirm what's going on here. You do understand that playing with tackychemistry is very illegal—in *every* jurisdiction."

It's feeling like we may be at the end of the road for the Bells' grand adventure, maybe even for their freedom. The question is, will I let that happen? What does my internal Gallie think? She's being suspiciously silent on the matter. I think about the photographs Alfie had mentioned—maybe images of other realities, other worlds. And I wonder what, who, those worlds might contain. Gallie is still being stubbornly quiet, so I remove the pistol from the back of my belt, rack it, and point it at the man carrying the holstered gun. It seems his face *can* display emotion.

The tall one speaks. "Don't be—"

"Alfie, the tough guy in the suit is carrying a gun. Would you mind taking it from his holster? He won't be stupid enough to stop you." Alfie does not hesitate, pulling open his jacket and removing the pistol. "Their phones too."

"You're not thinking this through, Bevan," the tall one says, the pitch of his voice rising from the bass register he'd been affecting.

"Both of you, stand against that far wall." They hesitate with token bravado until my arched eyebrows convey the question of whether we really need to go through all of this. I turn to Khara. "Are there other accelerators here?" He shakes his head. "Then bring that one. Alfie, will you grab any hardcopy documents and electronic puterpads?" She runs bench to bench, gathering paper and computers. Then I gesture for Khara and Alfie to follow me as I back out the door, pistol trained on the intruders. I slam it closed and nod to Khara to lock it.

"You find that under the bar?" Alfie asks, pointing at the gun.

"Yes, a good precaution in this day and age."

Big mistake are the words being yelled repeatedly from inside.

Alfie's eyes suddenly widen in panic. "My mother." We sprint into the parking lot and I point my pistol at the gray SUV.

"What are you doing?" she asks.

"Taking out their tires."

"That's just a replica," she says. "Use this one."

12
Joad

Mo's cramped car has an overpowering smell of stale fast food. He ignores the one traffic light between the Merry Crab and the cottage, and in a matter of minutes we burst into the village, decelerating steadily until we come to a stop at the corner of the narrow lane that leads to the Bells' cottage. There are SUVs parked out front.

"Shit." I sweep empty fast food containers from the back seat and lean forward.

"What now?" Mo asks.

"They won't hurt her," I say. "Are there any project materials in the cottage?"

"No."

"Okay, this isn't my call, Alfie. What next?"

She covers her face with her hands, as if deep in thought, then says, "If we go in there the project is over. We get locked up and probably for a long time."

"Agreed," I say.

"You don't think Victoria will—" Mo says.

"No, I don't," Alfie says. "Not a word. She's good at not being able to communicate when she needs to be." She runs her palms up and down her thighs. "We'll come back for her, but after we're done. After the project is over."

That's all that Mo needs to hear before beginning to back up slowly.

"Where are we going?" I ask.

"My place," he replies. "I have another charged accelerator there."

"You've kept one at home? We agreed—"

"Yes, it turns out I'm an arse."

"But a lovely arse, Mo."

Mo Khara's Scalmere neighborhood is less picturesque. We park in the courtyard of a dilapidated two-level apartment block that looks like it had once been proudly modern. We wait in the car for him. If this were any major town, it'd show signs of vandalism, maybe worse, with bars over windows and metal shutters over doors. But so far, it seems Scalmere has fared better than Megara, Iowa.

Mo returns carrying a carboard box, which he puts in the trunk. "What now?" he asks.

"We need a safe place to be," Alfie replies. "A place we can plan our trip." It seems that a 'trip' is what we're now calling our blind jump into oblivion.

There's a silence and I gradually get the impression that I'm the one who's supposed to come up with a solution. "Okay, I know a place. A blast from your little accelerator is good for two people?"

Mo nods.

"*Che cavolo,*" shrieks the woman as a pan clatters loudly on the floor.

"It's Joad," I say, trying to recover quickly from the disorientation of the accel. "Sorry, Lucia."

Lucia Bruno is wide-eyed, clutching her chest. Her black hair hangs in runnels and coils, accentuating her olive skin and brown eyes. "That could have fucking killed me, Joad. Why the hell are you acceling into my apartment?" Then she surveys my companions.

"We needed somewhere safe to be."

After a moment she catches her breath. "Safe? And you chose Paris?"

"I had your co-ords," I say.

"Oh, that's the reason. What a nice compliment. And why do you need somewhere safe? The last I heard you were a respectable college professor somewhere."

"It's a long... no actually, it's quite a short story." I introduce Alfie and Mo, although Alfie seems too mesmerized by the view from the large plate-glass window to notice. Dead center is an unobstructed view of the Eiffel Tower. The large, open-concept penthouse is stunning. Its white grand piano, pale wood sideboards with hand-carved inlays, chesterfield couches, and marble-topped kitchen counter are among other exhibits of unabashed opulence.

"Lucia was a colleague at TMA," I say.

"TMA paid better than I thought," Alfie says as she walks to the window and looks down on the 16th arrondissement. I had never been so indelicate as to ask Lucia how she'd acquired her wealth, but TMA operatives were generally presented with many opportunities to take a bauble here and there.

"Mind if we stay for a while?" I ask.

Lucia shrugs. "When have I ever said no to Joad Bevan?"

13
Joad

Throughout the next week we spend most of our time hunched over the dining table, scribbling notes and tapping into puterpads. Alfie insists that I be involved in verifying the calculations she and her mother had done—the ones that supposedly validate the required koson fluxes and chemical-reaction parameters. Notwithstanding the common wisdom that a theoretical physicist's mind flames out around their thirtieth birthday, the high stakes demand I make the effort to relive my better years. Mo's resentment of me is still strong, but he has more sense than to express a full-throated complaint in front of Alfie. From what I've learned so far, I second Mo's judgment. Lucia hasn't expressed much interest in what we're doing, or maybe she just understands that sometimes ignorance is the safest course.

Each night, after long hours of work, we look down at the gatherings on the streets below—mainly kids getting drunk, shouting at each other, smashing windows. One night they'd set a few cars alight, but neither the police nor the pompiers showed themselves. They probably decided that both the kids and the cars would burn themselves out. And if this very upmarket part of Paris is unprotected from the turmoil, the other parts of the city must be in abject chaos. All of this because of the callous physics that allows the mutation of timelines.

I'd occasionally see Alfie staring off into the mid-distance. I suggested once that we could call this off and go back to find her mother, but she hadn't considered that suggestion deserving of a response.

It's late and I'm losing focus so I join Lucia in the kitchen for a coffee top-up. "We'll be out of your hair soon," I say.

"No, that's not it. I like the company."

I smile as she pours my coffee.

"I hope you don't mind," she says, "but it's been hard not to overhear you now and again. I have a question for you."

I invite it with a nod. The hot coffee feels good on the back of my throat as I take my first sip.

"Are you out of your fucking mind?" she whispers. "Are you really going to let yourself get obliterated?"

"Yes and yes."

"To travel to another timeline, another reality? What does that even mean, Joad? Timelines aren't there to be traveled *between*. It doesn't even hold up as a concept, let alone a theory."

"And temporal physics *does*? I'm kind of used to things making no sense, Lucia."

"But at least—"

"I hear you, but the theory behind it is the most compelling—hell, exciting—thing I've seen in a long time. It's based—"

"Whoa, Joad. I was a TMA operative, not a scientist. Assume it'd be meaningless to me."

I watch Alfie and Mo as they work furiously, muttering numbers to themselves and occasionally at each other. Then I look at the glow from the window caused by the fires below.

Lucia breaks the silence and says, "There was a time this room would be flooded at night by the lights of the Eiffel Tower… bright as day. Tower got shut down long ago, and now all I see down there is the constellation of fires as the city burns. In a grotesque irony, Paris has become the city of lights."

"Are you safe here?"

"Oh, yeah. This place is a fortress, and the lobby is full of guards eager to try out the new assault rifles we bought them. All my supplies arrive by drone, so I don't leave the place much. Believe me, your company is welcome."

14
Joad

I leave Alfie and Mo to their sums and stop in at a local bar, which had raised its metal shutters for the evening. The Paris streets are relatively quiet for once and some of the residents are hazarding an outing, although I would have been willing to navigate riots just to get out. A couple cold beers go down well after being cooped up for days. Gallie hasn't visited me in a while now. My role in this global misery, my lost family, and the bitter realization that I've never been part of a meaningful success throughout my entire lousy career—none of these thoughts had summoned Gallie out of hiding. I notice that my fists are clenched, so I stretch my palms and take a deep breath. Since meeting the Bells, my life has become a dream sequence... not quite real. Is what I'm volunteering for no more than the opportunity to be dissolved in a mist of ultra high-energy particles?

What's more worrying is that I don't really care.

I notice a slender, fashionably-dressed woman ahead walking in my direction. She is what Parisians are supposed to look like. A moped ridden by someone dressed in black turns the corner behind her and mounts the sidewalk. He puts out a hand as he approaches her, and without stopping wrenches away her shoulder bag, causing her to fall forward onto her face. With glandular daring, I reach out as he passes me and grab the collar of his leather jacket, holding on with a death grip as his moped continues on without him, clattering behind me. His confusion turns quickly to rage as he gets to his feet, spitting words I don't understand as he lurches at me, fists clenched. With that much notice, it's easy to block his arm, and I deliver a gut punch, causing him to buckle forward onto his knees.

Then a second moped rounds the corner. Its rider dismounts and approaches me, waving a knife back and forth as if practicing his slash. I had once disarmed a thirteenth-century knight brandishing a broad sword, although in that case I'd had the advantage of a semi-automatic pistol, and of being much younger. I jump back, avoiding the arc of his slash, and then he regrips the knife, readying himself to deliver a downward stab. There's no way I can grab that arm without getting cut up, so I back away. He grins like an idiot villain, but then makes the mistake of glancing down at his friend to make sure he's witnessing my comeuppance. That's when I take a run at him, planting the sole of my boot squarely in the middle of his stomach, launching him backwards. As he hits the pavement I bring my heel down hard on his wrist, removing the knife from his grip. With force, I punch down onto his face. And again, and again. My mind has now left the fight, but my fist continues to pummel him. The blood spattering my knuckles may be his or may be mine as the blows raining down on him accelerate. Then I feel someone pulling on my shoulder, and I look up quickly, ready to redirect my attack. But it's the woman who had been their victim. She's shouting something… She's telling me to stop.

As the woman pulls me off my bloodied victim, I scan the street for his accomplice but he's gone. The remaining man's eyes are wide, his face barely recognizable, and he's staring up at me as if making sure his ordeal is over. I apologize, although I'm not sure to whom, then pick up her shoulder bag from the sidewalk and offer it to her, but she's not interested. She waves her hand for me to leave and I back away, then turn and walk off briskly. My body explodes in pain and I realize that my gallantry has duped me into thinking I'm a much younger man.

The guard on the apartment building steps inspects the pass Lucia had provided and then surveys me. He's wearing dark-blue fatigues with the word *SECURITÉ* emblazoned in yellow across his chest. An assault rifle hangs from his shoulder. He takes his time before opening the heavy oak door at the top of the steps, showing no curiosity about my heavily bloodied hand. One of the guards in the lobby is more inquisitive. "Que vous est-il arrivé, monsieur?"

"Agresseurs," I reply, and he gives me a knowing smile before calling the elevator.

I enter the penthouse suite to see Alfie sitting alone at the work table, staring into a puterpad screen. I have grown to be in awe of her energy, a level I had never experienced, even at her age.

"What the hell?" She's looking at my hand as I had forgotten my plan to conceal it in my pocket.

"Some kids thought they'd mug the old guy." This is almost true, and there's no need to mention that I had brought it on myself.

"Come on." She takes me to the kitchen to rinse the cuts, which hurts like hell, and then wraps a towel around my hand.

"Where's Mo?" I ask.

"With Lucia."

This takes a moment to register. "You mean…"

Alfie nods with a smirk.

"Wow. One of them is a quick worker."

"I don't begrudge any of us a little recreation. For you, it's beating up kids, for him, sex." She sits back down and waves me over. "I think we're nearly there, Joad. I'm feeling good with this. Are you?"

"Good? If you're asking whether I'm completely convinced we'll survive, then no. But that's too high a bar, I guess."

"What I meant was do you think we have the koson flux calibrations within an acceptable range? I already know you're not convinced we'll live through it. I think you've mentioned it once or twice."

The fact is, I don't have firsthand confidence in the calibrations, but I do have confidence in Alfie. "Then yes, I think we're getting there."

"We should be thinking about picking a destination in the neighboring timeline," she says. "We'll obviously use the minimum koson flux we think will get us to another timeline."

We don't have a meaningful definition of what a 'timeline close to ours' actually means, but that's where the minimum koson transition flux would theoretically take us. We'd also agreed that the first trip would be taken by only one of us because why risk three lives?

And I was to be the canary in the timeline.

15
Joad

There's a pall of general irritation hanging over us this morning. Alfie is squinting into her puterpad and shaking her head while Lucia clatters unnecessarily in the kitchen.

I start with Alfie. "Problem?" I need to repeat my question before she looks up.

She sighs. "Yes. Do you ever think you know which way a calculation is going, and then…"

"It doesn't?" Of course I do. It's the life of a theoretician.

She nods. "It's just something… I'll figure it out. Redo the whole bloody thing." Mo, looking over her shoulder, points at something on her screen, but Alfie bats his finger away. Meanwhile, Lucia is biting her fingernails.

"Is everything okay?" I ask. She looks at me without answering, forehead creased.

I'm about to turn back to Alfie when Lucia says, "Joad, what are you thinking?"

"Right now I'm wondering what the hell is going on today."

"Why are you doing this?" Now she has the attention of both Alfie and Mo. "Did you really think the DTS wouldn't have the technology to track your accel, all the way from origin to here? You know they can do that. Did you somehow think DTS would be too dumb to follow? You of all people should know better. It's what they do. You didn't even put a temporal component in your jump, which made tracking you even easier."

"What are you saying?" Alfie asks. "That they know we're here?"

"Of course they do. They contacted me the day you arrived."

Mo and Alfie stare at Lucia. "So why didn't they just follow us?" Mo asks.

"Because they want to understand what you're up to. Right now, I'm flashing back to just how street dumb TMA scientists always were."

"And you've been their spy?" Alfie says, her eyes widening with anger. "You picked a lovely girlfriend, Mo."

Lucia turns to me. "Joad, you know what they could have done to me if I'd told them to go fuck themselves. But it's what I wanted to say. Look, all I want is to live in my safe Paris apartment until I either croak or get screwed by a timeline transition. That's all."

I stare at Lucia. How did I not see this coming? The apartment must be laced with planted surveillance devices, which means the DTS could arrive in force at any moment.

"We leave, now," I say.

"But they'll just track us," Mo says.

"He's right," Lucia says. "Just let this go its course. They'll need you too much to harm you."

"They won't track us this time."

It takes a moment for Alfie to digest what I'd said. "No. Are you serious?"

The others look at her dumbly.

"But we don't have it all nailed down yet. Not after this morning's glitch!"

Mo is next to understand. "Are you insane? You want to make the jump right now? We'll kill ourselves."

"Let's just do it. If we don't, it'll never happen," I say, "and we'll be locked up for a long time, at the beck and call of the DTS. That's a lifelong nightmare."

There's a silence filled only by our thoughts until Lucia interrupts it. "You can't be seriously thinking about this."

Alfie grins, gesturing for Mo to hand her the two accelerators. "Okay, based on the latest analysis—for what it's worth…"

"For what it's worth," Mo echoes, shaking his head.

"I'm programming in the minimum koson flux."

"Whatever the hell that means," Mo adds.

"Put in another spacetime location too," I say. "No idea what the implications would be of landing us at the same spot."

"Yup," Alfie says as she prods the accelerator watches. "Don't want to meet ourselves and self-annihilate." She chuckles. It's not like our alternate selves will be made of antimatter, but we had discussed the unsettling scenario in which we meet ourselves a timeline away.

"This just gets better," Lucia says. "Mad. Completely mad."

Alfie takes a deep breath, straps on an accelerator, and hands the other one to me. Mo stares at it.

"I can't do this," he says. "I was always on board, you know that, Alfie, but only if we'd dotted all the i's and crossed all the t's. I'm not going to risk de-existing myself because we've done a half-arsed analysis. I have family, I…"

"I understand, Mo," Alfie says as we gather papers and puterpads into a pile.

I stare at the watch screen, in the middle of which is the *Activate* icon. Alfie and I glance at each other, more as a farewell than as encouragement.

"Joad, I'm sorry," Lucia says. "Just so you know, I didn't overhear anything I understood. Nothing… nothing to tell them. It was all just technobabble. And there were no bugs planted. Never in my apartment. No way."

Out of the corner of my eye, I see the agents pop in. And before I can hit the icon, I'm caught in an eye-lock with one of the half dozen people who are standing just feet away, all but one of them pointing a pistol at us. They seem to have suffered no disorientation—obviously not their first jump. I've been out of the game for far too long because, still startled, it takes me a full second to recognize Athol Green—the one without a weapon. The others are stony-faced agents in smart suits who give the impression that firing their weapons would not be an event of any significance to them.

I can't help but grin and Green reciprocates. "I didn't think you ever left your office, Athol. I feel special."

"Oh, Joad," he replies, "when someone with as high a profile in the community as yours does something this stupid, it deserves special attention."

"I see. Do they really have to be pointing those things at us?"

"Well, normally I'd have said no, but you've not been yourself lately."

"I tried to talk them out of this," Lucia says to Green, looking flustered.

"But I didn't ask you to," Green says. "In fact, I'm guessing you did a lot of talking I *didn't* ask you to do."

"She's an old TMA colleague, Athol," I say. "You know we look after each other. You're the exception more than the rule."

"I want you and Dr. Bell to hold out your arms, crucifix style," Green says. "Alfreda, I'm sure you want to be with your mother right now. She told me she'd like you back, sweet old thing."

I have a few seconds to convince myself that I have the advantage. If I press the *Activate* icon right now, events will be instantaneous since faster-than-light particles do not dawdle. Getting my right hand to the watch screen would be the main delay, but these goons wouldn't fire without Green's order. What happens after I activate the accelerator is a different matter. I glance at Alfie who's already looking at me. If I can make this calculation, then so can she.

I jab the *Activate* icon, and before the world around me evaporates, I hear Athol Green begin to shout out a loud exclamation, the end of which vanishes, along with the reality in which it was yelled.

16
Alt-Joad

I detect a fluttering between light and shade, and I can hear birdsong. I blink a few times before my focus returns: a canopy of broad leaves shifts in the breeze above me. Now the pain is registering. It's sharp and I touch the back of my head. No blood. I sit up slowly, trying not to inflame the already intense pain. Beneath the canopy is an understory of shorter trees, and below them, a lush undergrowth of large-leaved vegetation. I groan as I prop myself up, waiting for memories to return. Athol Green, Jeremy Chatham, an item exchanged, challenging them, then... Someone else had been there—someone with a heavy weight in hand.

I get to my feet, my head now threatening to explode. I scan the dense thicket of vegetation around me. It seems like the sort of place that something might suddenly burst out of the undergrowth. It could be a wild, fanged animal, an ancient armed to the gills, a reptilian meat-eater, or a tourist in a Hawaiian shirt and Bermuda shorts. A wave of nausea passes through me and I decide that sitting back down and taking a few deep breaths is the best decision, regardless of what may be out there.

So Jeremy Chatham has been leaking information to Athol Green? I had never understood Ria's confidence in that little shit. You could tell from across a crowded room that he didn't have a quark of sincerity in his entire body. Or of talent. And the vanishing of the Salkar refugee camp? Is that related? Is that where Green is sending information—a mole for the Zhirdikstanis?

Maybe my damaged brain is running amok. I check my pockets—all devices have been removed. There's nothing in the surrounding underbrush to recommend starting out in any particular direction. The pain that had been radiating from the back of my head now seems to be subsiding, replaced by a tingling in my bones, toes to teeth. The blow must have excited every nerve in my body.

I rise slowly, alert to the possibility of something big and dangerous, or small and poisonous, rushing at me as I push my way through the undergrowth.

Where the hell am I?

17
Joad

The comfortable temperature of the Parisian apartment is replaced by a cold breeze. This accel feels like the hundreds of others I've experienced... yet different. It's the same in that the scene before my eyes has vanished to be replaced by another; I now seem to be amidst a copse of trees swaying in the wind. It's the same in that there is no sensation of a journey—only the contrast between the beginning and ending environments: temperature, ambient light, background sounds, smells.

But it's different too. And it's different in a way that is difficult to pinpoint. A sense of mild nausea is one obvious distinction. And there's a tingling in my bones, my cheeks, my teeth. Those are not symptoms of a tachyon accel, no matter the expanse of time and distance that has been leaped.

I think to check that Alfie is still beside me, and she is. That's a relief. She's doubled over, hands on knees, like an athlete after crossing the finish line of a marathon. She nods that she's okay, then I remember to check on the stack of papers and puterpads piled between us.

"Where have you put us?" I ask.

"Scalmere. Contemporary."

I windmill my arms, hoping it will help the full-body tingle subside. In hindsight, there's no reason to expect that a koson wave would have the same effect on the human anatomy as a tachyon wave, and it could have been so much worse. We could have arrived as a pile of tingling bones.

"If we want to understand the differences between timelines, I thought I'd pick a familiar place," Alfie says, looking around us.

"Where now?"

Alfie takes a deep breath. "Okay, this way."

"First, let's dump the paper and puterpads. If someone catches us, I don't want them catching your work too. You have your reports on a needle drive?" She feels in her pocket, holds up the small stick, and puts it back. I look around and notice a chestnut tree with a sizable hollow. That's the place for our stuff, followed by a few handfuls of well-packed leaves.

We navigate out of the copse, holding back branches and cracking twigs under our feet. The path soon opens out into farmland with a view of the lake below. Before we get very far, Alfie halts in her tracks. "This is weird, we're going the wrong way." She looks behind her. "I'm really turned around here."

"So, which way?"

"I know these woods like the back of my hand. I've no damn business getting lost."

"So let's backtrack. Take the other way out of the woods." I turn to leave, but Alfie remains still, scanning the trees ahead.

"Sure, why not."

It takes just a few minutes to emerge once more from the woods, and this time we seem to be in the village of Scalmere.

"Shit," Alfie says from behind me. She's blinking rapidly as if that would reset the image before her. She's shaking her head. "This is… why does it look… I know this street, but…"

I notice something. "This isn't Scalmere, Alfie. We're not even in England. Look, the cars are driving on the right side of the street, the steering wheels on the left. Are we in North America? Europe? There are a lot of options for where we could be, but England is not one of them. Are you sure you programmed—"

"This is Scalmere, Joad. I grew up here so don't tell me we're not in Scalmere."

At the edge of the woods, I see a park bench facing the village and guide Alfie towards it. We sit and watch the passing cars. Then I notice something else. The signs on the row of village shops are not in Latin characters. No, wait, they are, but they're mirror-imaged. "The signs—"

"Oh shit. I know what's happening," Alfie says. As I start to ask what exactly she knows, she dismisses me with a wave of her hand. She obviously needs uninterrupted thought.

"We'd predicted it as a possibility," she says eventually, "but then actually seeing it…" She looks me in the eye. "The cars aren't driving on the right, the problem is us."

"Us?"

"We'd forecasted a theoretical scenario in which the paths between some timelines have the topology of a Möbius band—a path with a twist in it that inverts left and right between origin and destination. It's us who have been flipped, not Scalmere. So, because every aspect of our bodies, our brains, have been inverted, we see no difference in ourselves, and it's the external world that looks mirrored. Jeez, that's it."

I smile. I had not seen that one coming. "So navigation may be a challenge for us."

Alfie jumps to her feet. "We can deal with it. C'mon."

Alfie's confidence might have been misguided. It had been amusing to watch her thinking hard as we reached each street intersection. More than once, we'd backtracked after taking a turn. But it was surprising how quickly I learned to read backwards—at least short words. Other than the mirror inversion, the normality of this place surprised me, and I needed to remind myself that we were actually strolling through another reality. This is real life breathed into the mathematics that Alfie and her mother had laid out.

Despite Alfie's attempt to affect nonchalance, as we reach the corner of the lane leading up to the Bells' cottage, there is apprehension in her eyes. What will we find in that cottage? Will it be Victoria Bell? More troublingly, Alfie Bell? If we do find a Bell, would she be the same? Would she have an immediate understanding of who we are? We really have no idea of the extent to which this timeline differs from the one we left behind. So far, other than the embarrassment of having turned into our own reflections, the timeline seems identical. That does make sense because we'd used the minimum necessary koson flux predicted by the theory to get us between timelines.

We walk up the path to the front door, and if Alfie is noticing any anomalies, anything wrong, she isn't sharing it with me. She takes a key from her pocket but stops as she's reaching for the lock.

"It's different," she says. "It's not the right lock type."

I knock on the door as Alfie continues staring at the lock. I hear the patter of running feet and then the door opens. A small boy looks up at us, dressed in a heavy red sweater and pajama bottoms.

Alfie and I exchange a glance. "Is your mam here?" she asks. Then a young woman in a track suit appears, pulling the boy behind her.

"Yes?" she says curtly.

For a moment, Alfie seems lost for words. "Er... do you live here?"

"Yes."

"Sorry, sorry. Do you mind if I ask how long you've lived here?"

The young woman surveys us suspiciously. "My parents lived here."

"Do you know Victoria Bell?" I ask.

The woman shakes her head as she pulls the boy closer to her.

"Thank—" The door is slammed in our faces and we hear the young boy being berated. Alfie's eyes meet mine.

"There was no reason to expect an identical timeline," I say.

"No. Just a bit fucking unnerving."

"Look, we could pronounce the mission a success and go home… rescue your mother from whatever mess she's in. We've made the timeline transition, we've learned something about left-right parity inversion, we…"

Alfie's eyes are staring right through me; she's not listening. It's clear there's no way we're going home. "Okay, if your mother lives in town, someone at the Merry Crab is bound to know where, right? Dial us up a few tachyons and we'll pay a visit."

The pub snaps into view about fifty yards up the slope. It looks the same to me, and I catch up with Alfie who seems to have hit the ground in a brisk stride. As we approach, I notice a difference. The hanging sign, parsing the letters backwards, reads *The Highwayman*. Alfie has already entered the pub and I follow her.

Inside, it has the same look: oak posts and beams, and a shiny wooden bar with a rank of beer tap handles. Sitting at the tables are patrons, obviously dropped in for a lunchtime pint. On her way to the bar, Alfie waves at a couple of people but doesn't seem to be getting a response. I think I know what's coming.

"Is Toby working today?" she asks the barkeep, an older woman with crimson lipstick and big blond curls stacked high on her head.

"Who?"

"Toby McCallum."

"Toby McCallum? The lad who runs the ferry? He doesn't work here. What you 'avin?"

Alfie blows out her cheeks. "Do you know Victoria Bell?"

The barkeep considers the name and then shrugs.

I turn to face the patrons and call out, "Does anyone know Victoria Bell?" I hear a few giggles and one young guy in a baseball cap answers, "No, Tex. 'Ave you lost 'er?"

The barkeep testily asks us again what we want to drink. I grab Alfie's hand and lead her out of the pub, navigating the tables that are alive with bemused chatter.

"Hey, let's sit down for a minute," I say, guiding Alfie to an ancient stone wall that overlooks a field of grazing cows. "Let's take a breath, Alfie. If the Bells don't exist in this timeline, it's no big tragedy. Or mystery."

"That's a shitty thing to say." Her face has no sign of emotion. She picks up a rock from the top of the stone wall and hurls it into the field. "It feels weird."

"And maybe the Bells do exist, just not in Scalmere this time."

"Bells not in Scalmere? That's even weirder."

I smile as we breathe vapor into the chilly air. "Maybe we can find her. Tell me about your mom. There could be clues." Until that moment, having been so wrapped up in Alfie's family puzzle, I had forgotten about my own fantasy of finding Gallie here. "I know I'm no hero in Victoria's life."

"Oh, it wasn't just you. Her career at TMA was in the dumpster before you ever arrived on the scene."

"But I could have—"

"Stop wringing your hands. I'm not saying you weren't an arsehole, but if she hadn't quit TMA, a lot of good things wouldn't have happened. Like developing kosonics. That make you feel better?"

I have the sense that the question is not rhetorical, but I stay quiet.

"So what do you want to know about her? She was very depressed at TMA and made some stupid decisions. Me, for instance… I'm the product of a drunken one-night stand." She smirks. "Oh yeah, but in the end she made a good decision, at least good at the time. She quit TMA, we pulled up stakes and moved to a small town in west Africa where she taught science in a girls' school. And it was there she picked up the neuroparasite. So, no good deed goes unpunished, right?

"We moved back to her Scalmere roots, and after that it was me who became her life's work. Sent me off for an education, and then we picked the tachyon wall problem to start working on."

I simper. "Motivated by the great riches of the future if only you could cross it?" She gives me a searing glance. "Joking. I know that's not you."

The mystery of why there is a tachyon wall near the end of the twenty-first century—a barrier to time travel in both directions—had been mostly motivated by the prospect of bringing home the technological riches that likely exist on the far side. The commercial and military advantages of breaching the wall had been the dark fantasy of many a would-be magnate or dictator, although a few of us had had a purely academic interest.

"Anyway, failed on the wall problem of course, but it took us down an unexpected path to koson theory. Been working on that ever since."

"In complete isolation."

Alfie points at the pub. "She bought that place with her savings and worked there while she still could. The parasite took its sweet time frying her nervous system." Alfie's tone is quite matter-of-fact, not in the least mawkish.

"That's quite a story, Alfie." I throw a rock that lands beside hers. "Let's see if the Victoria of this timeline is findable. Agreed?" I sense this is exactly what we were about to do anyway.

She nods. "Yeah, it'll give us a chance to get a wider view of mirror world here."

"There could be a million explanations of why the Scalmere locals don't know the Bells, but it seems there's one obvious one. Say Victoria never left TMA. Never returned to Scalmere and lived here so long ago that no one we've asked remembers her."

"Go on."

"What if she even stayed with TMA long enough to take the career jump to DTS? In that scenario she might still work for the department."

"In Risley?"

"That's where any DTS scientist with at least half a brain would work. Worth a shot?"

Alfie nods.

I point at her wrist accelerator. "I can give you coordinates."

18
Joad

The semi-arid landscape of eastern Washington state with its parched grass and golden sagebrush appears before me, the foothills of the Cascades looking like giant stuffed pillows. If I've remembered the coordinates correctly, we should have landed just outside the tachyon shield protecting the DTS site, and the bow wave from our accel will certainly have caught someone's attention. I turn to see the site fence and, in the distance, the large, inelegant structures that house the DTS acceleration and detection facilities. Two gate guards are making their way towards us, weapons in hand.

"I'll handle this," I say, more to reassure myself than her. Then one of the guards breaks out into a broad grin.

"Dr. Bevan." He lowers his rifle. "Where's your car?"

I don't know what this means. Does this guy remember me from back in the day? He looks much too young for that. But in this familiar environment, it's easy to forget we're in an alien world. Maybe here I still work for TMA... DTS.

"Hi there," I say, affecting a familiarity which I hope is not too much. "How's it going? Yeah, car problems." The guards look at Alfie but say nothing. So what next? *Does*

Victoria Bell work here? seems too blunt, especially since this may be 'my' workplace.

"Secretary Galois has been calling the gate this morning to ask if we've seen you."

My body freezes and my breathing stops. I ask him to repeat what he'd just said, and he does. *Secretary Galois?* No. Gallie had quit the TMA long before her life had been vanished in the timeline switch. Two of us dealing with TMA politics had seemed like more than a healthy marriage could bear. But here, not only does she work for the DTS but she's the secretary? And I work for them too? Who *are* these people?

"We'll drive you to the facilities, sir," the guard says.

I thank him. "Left my credential in the car, I'm afraid. We'll both need visitor passes."

I don't cope with the unexpected the way I used to. In my TMA years, which are now rushing back at me, it had seemed that my job description was to stand at the receiving end of a tsunami of surprises. But now that I've softened, my heart is pounding as I open the door to the detection hall. It won't be Gallie, not my Gallie, will it? She'll be someone else in a way that I don't even want to think about.

I look around, and but for the mirror effect and a few details, the hall is just as I remember it: a labyrinth of cubicles in front of a glass wall, behind which is the monitoring room with its rows of terminals and a large screen displaying accelerations around the globe. But now the screen is just one large blotch of green—more accel events than they could possibly do anything about. Are they tracking them just out of curiosity?

I'm told that Secretary Galois is in one of the apartments, and I know which one. It's the one in which we have history… I think. I sit Alfie down in a cubicle. She looks around herself agog, perhaps a little wonderstruck by the reality of a place her mother must have described to her.

She has her own family mystery to solve, but at this instant, that's not top of my mind.

I stop in front of the apartment door and try to control my breathing. When I open it, the woman facing me is Gallie... Jane Galois... Gal. All my mind and body are allowing me to do is to stare. I realize my mouth is agape and quickly shut it. I need to keep it together. I need to be the Joad she knows, but who the hell is that?

"Where the fuck have you been?" she says.

I thought I remembered her voice, but now it has a familiarity beyond my imperfect memories. It's husky but precise, and warm around the edges. Her face is expressing anger but it belies amusement in her bright eyes. "Out on a bender with an old school friend?" I'm too stupefied to smile. "You're lucky I'm not the suspicious type."

I'm staring but she'll just have to get used to it. Her hair has turned from gray to pure white, but otherwise she's the Gallie I'd lost.

"You look different," she says. "Are you going to say something?" I'm still struggling to find words. She's scrutinizing me, not with suspicion but with curiosity. Do I look different to her? Is it because of the peculiar mirror in which my body is reflected? After all, no face is perfectly left-right symmetrical. Or maybe it's something more mundane. Perhaps I'd had a beard or put on fifty pounds.

"Why are you wearing your wedding band on the wrong hand? You really have been hitting on old flames, haven't you?" I'm about to protest when a grin consumes her face. "You're brave and adventurous, my lovely husband, but you're not stupid."

I need to say something but my mouth won't comply. My voice may not sound right. I might sound like an alien impersonating Joad Bevan. I muster the will to whisper "Gallie." Then I step forward and throw my arms around her.

"Hey, don't break me, I—"

I kiss her. It's a long kiss, and after our lips finally separate, she whispers, "What the hell happened last night? Are you okay?"

"Very okay," I whisper back. "Is Casy okay?"

She pushes me back by my shoulders. "Why? As far as I know he is." I shake my head and smile. Then she says, "And why *is* this ring here? You do need to explain that, Joad."

"Oh yes, Gal. Explanations are coming your way." I take her hand and lead her to the detection hall. Her hand is real and warm—not the imaginary hand I had been holding for years.

Alfie sees us approaching and stands.

"Alfie, this is… this is my wife, Jane Galois." Gallie shakes Alfie's hand and looks at me with growing suspicion. "And this is Alfreda—"

"I'm Alfie." She has a look that tells me she's not yet ready to be on last-name terms.

"And who is Alfie?" Gallie asks.

Alfie takes something from her pocket and hands it to Gallie. It's the needle drive. It seems that this is how Alfie wants to make her introduction, so I wait for her to explain. The silence makes it clear that that job is being delegated to me.

"Gal, there's a lot to discuss, but first, we need you to digest the report on that needle drive."

Gallie's brow furrows. "Is this more important than our towering priority?"

I don't know what that is, but I'm sure the right answer is *yes*. "Trust me, Gallie, it's important. And give a copy to your best theoretician."

Gallie shrugs, glances over my shoulder and calls out to someone. "Ria."

The woman coming towards us is broad-shouldered, statuesque, and walks with the smooth, confident gait of an athlete. I had not remembered Victoria Bell looking like an Olympian.

I turn to Alfie and the shake of her head is almost imperceptible. *Not now.*

"You'll need an hour to get first impressions of what's on there," I say. "Let's talk after that. Oh, and it's possible you may need to mirror-invert the coding. You'll figure it out."

Gallie casts Ria a bemused glance. "It'd better be special, Joad," Gallie says, tossing the drive to Victoria Bell.

19
Joad

Alfie and I are sitting in the cafeteria eating sandwiches that may have been in the vending machine since I last worked here. If Alfie had been traumatized by seeing Ria, she's concealing it well. This is a stoic, no-nonsense woman and I wonder if it's just what women from the north of England are like.

"Well, we've solved the mystery of Victoria," I say. "At least part of it. Does she look the way she used to before… the illness?"

"It's… need time to think this through." We sit quietly, chewing old meat in stale bread. "When they read the report, they may just say 'Yeah, we know all this. What's your point?'"

"Maybe."

"And my… Ria didn't notice me. I'm guessing that I don't exist in this timeline, otherwise…"

"Maybe."

"Is 'maybe' going to be your end of this conversation?" She throws her sandwich down and I do the same. "And when you asked this Gallie to give the report to her best theoretician, she called that Ria over. *Best theoretician* is not a role my mother was recognized for in TMA. Not many even knew her name. And…"

"And what?" Alfie shakes her head, but I insist.

"Just a philosophical point, so pretty meaningless. But would we say that Ria is really my mother? Even if there were a version of me in this timeline, would she be *my* mother? Is this Gallie *your* wife?"

The question takes me by surprise, the most surprising aspect of it being that I hadn't already posed it to myself. Of course Gallie's my wife. That's Gallie. My Gallie. How could that be in doubt. But then, what might the local Joad Bevan say about that?

"Right now, I wish I were in the Crab cozying up to a beer tap."

"I know what you mean," Alfie says, and she begins to drum her fingers on the table.

Ria shows us into a cramped space where Gallie is already sitting. In an age where paper is almost defunct, they have somehow achieved the look of a major city library before any of the books have been shelved. Ria points to two metal-framed school chairs and we sit down.

There's a silence and I sense them considering where to start. Their expressions are ones you'd have if a shih tzu had just gotten on its hind legs and written the Maxwell equations on a whiteboard.

Gallie speaks first. "Where's it from? The paper?" She turns to Alfie. "Were you involved in writing this?"

Alfie nods.

"Who are you with? Which organization?"

Alfie casts me a glance before answering. "I'm not with any organization."

Ria leans forward. "You're saying this is your work? You wrote this?"

Alfie studies Ria's expression of incredulity. "There's one other author," she says. "And yes, we worked alone.

Nothing fucks up creativity like working in a large organization of talented peers."

In Alfie there is a younger me, yet far worse. It's the view that everyone you encounter is visiting from the far reaches of the bell curve. I notice that Ria is smiling, which licenses me to do the same. Gallie turns to me with an expression that conveys I'd better be the one who starts talking sense.

"Joad," she says with a dangerous smile, "are you going to make us guess the right questions to ask, or are you just going to tell us what the hell is going on here?"

"I will, Gallie, but first, what do you make of it? The paper?"

Gallie and Ria glance at each other. "I'd say it's a breakthrough," Gallie says. "We need to digest it more, but I'd say it's a real advance… a foundational advance."

Ria nods her agreement. "To put it mildly, yes. But I find it hard to believe that this originated outside of any research institution we know of."

Gallie looks at me. "Effon theory, or more accurately, the gap that is effon theory. Does this fill it? Is that what you think?"

Effon theory means nothing to me and my face must show it, so she adds, "That effons are kosons would be convenient, wouldn't it?"

I nod reflexively.

"So now explain," Gallie says. "Why has this come at us out of the blue?"

"Not the blue, exactly," I reply. "You've read the final section of the report? The engineering applications?"

Ria and Gallie are momentarily nonplussed but then Ria's eyes open wide. "No… No. Are you saying… are you saying that Alfie here was wafted to us on a koson wave?"

I look at Alfie for permission and she nods. "Yes," I reply, then turn to Gallie. "And not just Alfie."

20
Alt-Joad

The only sign of animal life so far has been the symphony of birdsong and the brattling of some kind of insect. I had traveled once to the Cretaceous period and the vegetation here reminds me of it, but I'm hoping that that's as far as the similarity goes. I'm not hearing the roars of something big and hungry or feeling the ground tremors of something massive, so I'm choosing optimism. I've been walking for what seems like a couple of hours, my progress through the thick undergrowth slow. It's been getting hotter since I set out and sweat is dripping from my nose.

As the vegetation and canopy begin to thin out, I find myself looking down onto a shallow, tree-lined valley with a meandering river running along it. The sun is getting lower in the sky and I need to squint into it to track the course of the valley to the horizon. There's a heat haze. I can't be exactly sure what I'm seeing but in the distance something looks human-made. It might be a small collection of buildings—perhaps a settlement of some kind. But a settlement of what, of who? I decide to track the valley via the forest on its slope, having had some experience of human settlements that take a dim view of strangers. Maybe

I'm wrong, and maybe I'll be greeted with cocktails and canapés, but I've found that scenario to be more the exception than the rule.

After one or two more hours of creeping progress, the jungle terrain transforms into what looks more like the undergrowth of a temperate forest. The trees are taller and seem more familiar, maybe firs and spruces, and the birdsong is less exotic, less tropical. I approach the tree line where the forest terrain gives way to the valley slope, and take in the view of the settlement. This time I can discern individual structures, people moving around, although they are too distant to make out their attire.

There's a familiarity in what I'm seeing, and then there's an instant of recognition. I stare, unblinking. It looks like the Salkar refugee camp—the one we'd seen vanish. The thought that occurs to me is one that should have dawned much earlier. I'd been assuming that what had sent me here was a tachyon accel. But maybe it had been something else. If someone just wanted to get rid of me without a trace—someone with the means of making effons—wouldn't they take advantage of that technology? Why risk a tachyon accel that could be detected and tracked? But if all they have is what Chatham leaked to them, they'd have no clue about... this.

Whatever this is. As far as they know, I, like the Salkar community, would have simply been annihilated.

Have I just connected two dots, or am I delirious? It'd be nice because otherwise I'm adrift in a constellation of isolated, disjointed dots. I sit down, propping myself against a tree to watch the refugees going about their business. Then I notice something strange, even by the standards of recent events. I creep a few steps down the shallow incline of the valley for a better view. It's the people... their motion. They seem to be extremely energized and running about the site. But it isn't that they're running, it's just that they have a rapid, jerky motion that reminds me of an early twentieth-century movie being played back too fast.

TIME WALL

Time dilation? That's what it would look like. For some reason, their clock is ticking faster than mine? But the settlement is maybe a mile away, so that's impossible. I duck my head into my bucket of weird physical phenomena, which has become ever deeper over the years, but surface with nothing. The only effect I can think of that's possibly relevant is gravitational time dilation—time slowing down near the event horizon of a black hole, but I'm certainly not feeling the body-ripping tidal forces that'd come with being near a black hole.

Then I have another random thought. I remember from my post-doc days doing some work on hetero-temporal spaces. These were hypothetical places where time passes at different rates depending on where you're standing, but there was no real physics behind any of that. It was just a mathematical curiosity we played around with.

I look up the valley to where I'd first emerged from the jungle. A flock of birds is soaring high above it, or at least that's my first impression. In fact, every bird in the flock is static—essentially frozen in the sky. At least almost frozen. Well, if I were to believe in my post-doc shenanigans, I'd say there is what we would have called a temporal gradient running along the direction of the valley.

Where the hell am I?

21
Joad

At first, Gallie has no words. I tell our story—most of it, at least—and her reaction is just to stare at me, and then at Alfie.

"I'd say you were losing your mind," she finally says. "If I hadn't read the paper, that's what I'd say." Ria is studying her computer screen, which I assume is displaying the report. "So what you're saying is that you're not... *my* Joad?"

I'm awash with hurt and confusion. She's right, but every emotional fiber in me is telling me that there's a Joad and there's a Gallie, and here we are, together, each other's. She can't reject me. I don't think I could bear that.

"And the ring on the wrong hand? Are there different conventions in your universe?" Gallie asks with a wry smile.

"Möbius inversion," Alfie says matter-of-factly. This gets Ria's attention. "You won't find it in there," Alfie says, nodding at Ria's puterpad. "Not an intrinsic part of the model but we knew it was a possibility. Nothing to stop it. You probably noticed its effect in the needle drive data."

Ria surveys Alfie carefully. She may be just digesting the point, but maybe it's more... I don't know why Alfie is choosing to keep her little secret from Victoria, but it's her call. Maybe she wants to ration the trauma.

Gallie shakes her head as if making way for new thoughts. "But if you're not... where is *my* Joad? He went out to get some air last night... drove downtown." Gallie turns away from me. Am I evoking all the wrong emotions? Me, the imposter.

"Last I heard from him... the other Joad... was late last night," Ria says. "He called me."

Gallie's jaw drops. "What? You're telling me this now? Where was he? What did he want?"

"Sorry, Gallie, I'd forgotten about it, and then... this Joad showed—"

"Need an answer."

"He was asking if Athol Green was in Risley. Don't know where he was calling from."

"And is he?"

"I made an inquiry and let him know that Green wasn't in town. Sorry, Gallie."

"And why the hell would Green be in Risley? He didn't say why he wanted to know?"

Ria shakes her head.

"And you didn't ask?"

I'm sensing that Green is a prick in more than one timeline.

"It was the middle of the night. I didn't—"

"For heaven's sake, Ria."

I remember well this small apartment on the TMA site. Gallie and I have history here, although not this Gallie, not with this Joad. She's sitting on the corner of the bed deep in thought. I sit by her and reach for her hand, but she withdraws it and slides away from me. I'm not her Joad, and I don't see myself being able to cope with this. Despite expectations that are now embarrassing, the reason Gallie led me to the apartment was to have a place to talk alone.

"Joad, I'm not sure what to say to you. I'm sorry that your timeline shifted and that I... your Gallie... was taken from you. But I'm not her. You see that, right? At least I don't think so, and I need some time to process this."

"Good luck with that, Gal." I move to the chair by the bed.

"So Joad rang Ria in the middle of the night to ask whether Athol Green was in town, and then he never came back."

"And I show up."

"Yeah, you show up. *Mirror man*."

We stare at each other, but I have nothing to offer.

"I've arranged us an accel to DC," Gallie says. "A word with Dr. Green is warranted."

"Yes. If he's got something to do with... Joad vanishing, then I think he'll be a bit perturbed to see me."

Gallie nods. "I'm a little overloaded right now. Understand, I know that koson theory and the whole you and Alfie thing should be front and center for me, but..." She exhales through puffed cheeks. "I'm leaving Ria to hash out the paper with Alfie. That's on Ria's plate for now, not mine."

"I have a feeling that Ria is going to latch onto it pretty quickly," I say.

"So, in DC, as you're playing Joad Bevan, there's something to understand."

I give her a wry smile. "A role I was born to play."

"No one outside Ria's group is aware of our effon experiments, or even of the existence of effons."

"Kosons."

"Right. We need to better understand all of this before we add another dimension—literally—to the gross confusion. Until you showed up, we had no reason to assume that a koson flux did anything but annihilate."

I know Gallie—and maybe even this one—but if she's been withholding information from her bosses, I doubt that avoiding more confusion is her real motivation. "A weapon. That's where they'll go," I say.

"Do you know how long after the discovery of nuclear fission it was when they detonated the first nuclear weapon?" Gallie asks. "Less than seven years. That was the time from breakthrough to weaponization."

"Probably take much less than that to get a koson bomb."

Gallie rubs her temples. "What worries me is that that weapon has probably already been used—that some foreign power has happened upon the same phenomenon we did." Gallie then describes a classified video of a vanishing refugee camp. "We can't come up with any other explanation for it."

"Well, the silver lining is that if that event was really a koson blast, then I'm the evidence that annihilation was likely not the outcome."

I sense from Gallie's unfurrowing brow that she had not thought of that. "No, maybe not," she says.

It's an unrelated, pathetic, and overpowering thought, but I wonder if she'd let me kiss her, just for old time's sake. Shame washes over me, and I suddenly feel like a predator. This is brutal, and I really do miss the good old days when the most unsettling mystery was mere time travel.

I lift my wrist and look at my accelerator watch. A crash course from Alfie on how to program this clever little thing seems like a timely idea.

22
Alt-Joad

I continue along the valley slope in the direction of the camp, and as I'd predicted, the fast, jerky motion of its inhabitants is becoming less pronounced—slowing down—as the tick rates of our hypothetical clocks become closer and the time dilation effect decreases. I descend the slope, realizing that I must by now be visible to someone in the camp.

As I'd remembered, the camp is composed of structures fashioned from scrap materials, tents, and now with the addition of a few log cabins. Two men approach, their rifles trained on me, and I raise my hands, affecting a stupidly innocent smile. They do not reciprocate, and one shouts out in a language I don't understand. They both have long, straight black hair and heavy beards, and are wearing T-shirts and jeans. The one who'd said something before repeats it, this time with thinning patience.

"I'm sorry, I don't understand you," I call back, and the two men exchange a glance.

"English?" the other one asks.

"American." Unless my geopolitics is way off, the US has been supportive of the Salkars while the Zhirdikstanis are trying to round them up and expel them.

"Identification?" he asks.

I shake my head. "I have nothing."

He pats me down for weapons as the other man targets my chest. Then he beckons me to follow and we descend into the camp. From this elevation, I can see it covers an area of maybe two hundred by two hundred yards. We walk past an animal carcass, mainly bones and rotting muscle, its head covered by a sheet.

Now I'm getting the attention of the camp residents, who are stopping their work or play to survey me. Construction is underway throughout the camp with more log cabins being erected, obviously to replace the shoddy structures that had arrived with them. We stop in front of a cabin. As I wait for the guard to return, a small child throws a pebble at me and laughs before running away. The guard re-emerges and beckons me to enter.

The interior looks more Paul Bunyan than Salkar. Standing behind a crudely hewn wooden table are two tall women, maybe in their thirties, one dressed in a colorful but threadbare chapan, the other in jeans and a loose denim shirt. Both have long black hair, high cheekbones, and dark eyes that are scrutinizing me. Against each wall is a guard, one rifle between the four of them, the others carrying large curved blades in their belts. The woman in the chapan beckons me forward.

"American?" she says in a low register that's heavily accented.

I nod. "American."

"Where in America are you from?" the other woman asks with a crisp diction.

I tell her Washington state.

"Where in Washington state?" Her accent sounds North American. Maybe I'm being tested.

"A little town called Risley in the east of the state."

"How you get here?" the woman in the chapan asks.

I smile. "I don't know. And I'm guessing you don't know how you got here either."

The women exchange a brief glance. "What's your job?"

Answering this will take some thought, but I doubt I can afford any delay. Saying I work for the United States government could elicit a range of possible responses. I'm almost certain that the US had formally admonished the Zhirdikstanis for their treatment of the Salkars, but also that we had not done a hell of a lot about it. I decide to resort to honesty as I wouldn't know how to optimize a lie. "I work for the US Department of Temporal Security."

The woman with the American accent flashes a faint smile. "And how temporally secure are you feeling at this moment?"

"More than I have in a while," I reply. "But the bar is low."

She nods. "We're being rude, what's your name?"

"Joad Bevan."

"I'm Ayana. This is my sister Sofia."

I smile, but sense as I scan the room that this growing intimacy is not widely welcomed: One of the guards is holding the hilt of his dagger and the one with a rifle is seeing no reason to lower it.

"What do you last remember before you arrived here?"

"I remember a blow to the head, and then here I am, a few miles downriver."

She approaches me and adjusts the hair on the back of my head. "That must have hurt, Joad Bevan."

The woman called Sofia says something over her shoulder, which prompts a man and a woman to enter, both very old and wearing ripped chapans, the man in a karakul hat. She invites me to sit, then barks out something at the guards, which does not seem to sit well with them. She repeats it, this time more forcefully, and they glower at me as they exit the cabin.

The food served by the old couple is very welcomed. I stuff cold meat and some kind of white vegetable stalks into my mouth too quickly to taste.

"Am I eating meat from the carcass outside?"

"A lot of carnivores come to visit us," Ayana says, "and the hunter usually becomes the prey."

"What was it?"

"I don't know exactly. We don't catalog them, we just eat them. I'd say it was some kind of ancient mammal if it weren't for the fact that it's here now."

Sofia is eating with gusto, happy just to listen to the conversation.

"Speaking of now, you must have noticed the time dilation effect."

"The…?" Ayana's brow furrows. "Oh, that things quicken up as you look west, but then seem normal once you get there? You mean that?"

I nod.

"Yeah, no clue what's going on. I studied art history at Stanford."

"Hence the accent." I wash down the meat with water and sit back in my chair, sated. "Thank you." I nod at the two old servers who seem uncomfortable with my gratitude. "I didn't study art, but I'm still at a bit of a loss. It's a temporal gradient of some kind. The further west you travel, the faster the ticks of the proverbial clock. But you're not aware of it once you get there because you become part of it."

"Well, we tend to stay local, although we do have visitors now and then."

"People?"

"No, you're the first. You've caused quite a buzz."

"So, with that beast out there, I'm guessing it arrived from the east—from a place where time has been too sluggish to let evolution get on with it?"

Ayana shrugs. "Impolite to ask."

"If it's true, it means you could take a hike eastward into… I don't know… the Cretaceous."

"Do you think?"

"Maybe not. I don't know shit at the moment, Ayana."

She sits quietly, digesting my ramblings. "Do you want to see the camp?"

There is an air of squalor, maybe because they're keeping the camp tight for protection. Spaces have been cleared for the construction of cabins, but it feels haphazard, with no obvious logic to the layout of the tents and scrap metal structures. With the dense forest above the valley, they have no shortage of building materials. I seem to be an object of intense curiosity; some of the villagers stare at me with suspicion, and others openly laugh as they exchange observations. Ayana has to shoo away some kids who have started to run up and touch me.

"How long ago did you arrive here?" I ask.

"Six months, maybe."

I estimate that by my personal clock and the date stamp on the satellite imagery I'd seen, this camp had vanished just a few days ago, but that seems consistent, maybe, with the time dilation. "It looks like your conditions here are an improvement."

"Does it? It's not the life we lived before we were rounded up and put in camps," she says, maintaining a smile that worsens my surge of embarrassment. "We lived the lives of modern people. The couple who served you food—before the purge, he was a veterinary surgeon and she was a lawyer."

"I'm sorry."

"Why are *you* sorry?"

"What did you and your sister do before…"

"Sofia was active in politics, and now she's our mayor—the only one of us who got a promotion out of all this." Ayana smiles.

"And you?"

"I'm afraid I was a serial academic, mostly in the US living off grants and killing myself by degrees. At least until the world started burning, and then I came home."

An animal that looks like a sheep, except for its curled, oversized horns, approaches us, bleating a complaint about our intrusion.

"That's Nuri. He showed up one day," Ayana says, reaching out to stroke him. "Do you really have no idea how we got here?"

This swerve puts me off balance. "Well, I can guess. I think we were the victims of a weapon that someone thought was some kind of death ray, but it turns out that it wasn't."

"And the Zhirdikstanis have that weapon?"

"If I'm right, they must."

She ponders this as she curls her long dark hair around a finger. Gallie does that same thing when she's deep in concentration, but I can't let my mind go there… not yet.

"What do the Zhirdikstanis have against you?" she asks.

I shrug. "I think they're not the only ones with such a weapon."

23
Joad

We stand shivering in the chilly DC air as we look across K Street into the warm glow of a restaurant. Athol Green is dining alone, as we were told he would be, fork in one hand and phone in the other, probably scrolling through the day's political machinations. Gallie and I have scouted the restaurant and its surroundings, and are now ready to deploy our half-formed plan for a frank conversation with Green.

I cross the road, enter the restaurant, and without missing a stride, approach his table. I sit down and he looks up, a momentary delay in recognition. I smile at him, and his eyes open wide as he drops his fork and begins to choke. It's a satisfying reaction. Then he looks around frantically, as if I may have brought backup with me.

"How did you…?"

"How did I what, Athol? How did I get back? Is that what you're trying to ask?" I hand him his water and he splutters into it. "We need a heart-to-heart, you and me. Let's go somewhere quiet." I stand up but he doesn't move. "I don't think you're in any position to be troublesome, are you, Athol? C'mon."

He slowly gets to his feet and follows me to the corridor that's signposted for the rest rooms. I push open the door at the far end, which I know leads to the back alley, and push him up against the wall. My face is close to his, my hands on his shoulders.

"Okay, Athol, now's the time to explain."

Before I can get an answer, he pushes me hard and I trip backwards, banging my elbows against something as I try to cushion my fall. "Well, right," I say, getting to my feet. "You're making this a lot easier for me."

He flinches as if I had already launched a blow. Not to disappoint, I deliver a fist to his stomach and follow it with a punch to the jaw, which causes him to crumple against the wall. I shake the pain off my hand, bending down to continue the conversation. "I'm ready for the full explanation. Don't make me hurt myself."

He wipes his sleeve across his face, checking it for blood, of which he finds plenty, then looks up at me. "Fuck you," he says before spitting out a mouthful of blood.

I use his tie to pull him to his feet.

"You know, as a traitor, your future is bleak," I say. "But believe me, the bleakest part is the next sixty seconds."

"Traitor? You call me a traitor?" His bloody grin is grotesque. "Chatham and I are the patriots. You and your wife, in your little exclusive cabal—*you're* the traitors. Who are you to conceal information from the White House—things that affect national security? Who the hell do you think you are?" He spits out more blood and I step back. "What disappoints me is that a blast of your fucking effons didn't deal with you for good."

Gallie appears from behind the dumpster, and as I turn to her, Green makes a dash for it down the alley. I start to pursue him until I hear Gallie calling me back. Her face is partly in shadow, but I see distress in it. She seems to be verifying her own logic before she speaks.

"The information Chatham's been supplying—Green wasn't passing it to a foreign power, he was passing it up the command chain."

I look down the alley but Green is long gone.

Gallie's office in Risley replaces the alley in front of me, and I quickly check that she's still by my side. It's a relief as I wasn't sure I'd understood Alfie's programming instructions. While I'm still processing what's just happened, Gallie is already leaning into her desk communicator to summon Ria and Alfie.

"My guess," she says, "is that Joad, my Joad, saw something he shouldn't have, and that won him a koson ride."

My Joad. I'll just live with that for now. Maybe I'm only a sad mirror image of the real thing, but as far as I'm concerned, the woman I'm looking at right now is my Gallie.

Moments later, Ria and Alfie burst in.

"In the very near future, Joad and I are going to be *personae non gratae*," Gallie says, "so we need to be elsewhere."

"What—" Ria doesn't get her question out.

"I'm going to assume that Alfie will come with us," Gallie continues. "The question for you, Ria, is will you come or will you stay? I'm afraid explanations are for later."

"Come, of course," Ria replies without hesitation. "But come where?"

"A tachyon accel will be traceable," I say. "But there's the other option." I raise my wrist.

"I thought you might suggest that," Gallie says, "but with all respect to you and Alfie, I'm not going to get swept up in a koson blast before I have a lot more understanding of what the hell it is."

"So what does that leave?" Alfie asks.

"Ria, is your car in the lot?"

She nods.

"We're going old-school. I'm assuming that only we know about Alfie's report?"

"Correct," Ria replies.

"Then I need you to do an unrecoverable delete of every on-site copy, except for Alfie's needle drive. Those bastards in the cabinet," Gallie murmurs. "They'd known about effons—kosons—ever since Chatham started feeding them information, which was probably right after we observed the anomaly. They also probably guessed that a koson event had vanished the Salkar refugee camp. So that whole charade of a meeting in the White House was just to put pressure on me to come up with an explanation of the physics so it could be used more effectively, efficiently. And you can be damn sure that weaponization is top of their minds."

24
Alt-Joad

It's early but too cold to get back to sleep, so I step outside my scrap metal shack and look down the slope toward the center of camp. It's quiet and deserted but for Nuri, the sheeplike animal, who is grazing by one of the cabins. A low-hanging mist gives the camp a ghostly quality, and the rising sun looks white and faded. I shiver as I trace the silver river along the valley until it disappears around a promontory. There's a lot to take in, human and physical, and maybe this early start is for the best.

How might a hetero-temporal landscape work? The abstract mathematical models of hetero-temporality I'd played with in my early research years had had no grounding in any real physics or version of reality, so none of that is helpful. What is the extent of a temporal zone? Are these zones confined to the surface of this... world, I assume? That'd mean the further west you travel, the longer the days would be, until you'd get to a point where the sun is almost frozen in the sky—near-perpetual day, or night. Or does it work differently from that?

What the hell is this place? That's the real question.

TIME WALL

I do miss my youth and my academic days where physics all seemed so wrapped up—or most of it, at least. Sure, we had people mucking around with superstring theory and quantum theories of gravity, but none of that affected real lives. It was the concern of a handful, and far from a matter of life or death. People didn't riot on the streets because some quantum theory was mathematically intractable.

I walk a few yards up the slope and cross the tree line, listening to the silence of the forest. It hurts me to think how worried Gallie must be by now, if we even share a *now*. Maybe Gallie is a billion years ago at this point, or maybe it's me who—

I hear something. A snapping branch. I look around but there's no sign of motion. As I turn to make my way back down to the camp, I see it, standing right in front of me. A mammal—maybe six feet high at the shoulders and twice as long. It looks front heavy with a long snout on a massive head that juts forward like a continuation of its thorax. It has a thin mane along its back and squat legs like a hippo. Slowly, it starts to circle me, its bovine eyes never leaving mine. I'm holding on to the possibility that this thing is strictly vegetarian, but then it bares its teeth, which look like long rows of three-inch daggers. It snaps its jaws at the air and I step backwards, looking frantically for something that might pass as a weapon. The only candidate is a fallen branch, and so I reach down slowly, keeping my eyes locked on the animal's, which now look decisively less cowlike. It edges towards me and I retreat, trying to maintain the distance between us. Then it snaps at the air again, and I raise the branch, pointing the sharper end at the animal, feeling more than hearing the low pitch of its growl.

My heart is hammering against my ribs, and then I'm suddenly gripped by an insane sense of amusement. This is how I go? Devoured by a species I don't recognize on a world that's even more ludicrous than the one I left behind? I'd always thought it'd be an inconvenient timeline shift that finally got me.

It turns away from me, as if contemplating whether its violent lifestyle is really necessary. But then it turns back and charges, vapor billowing from its wide-open snout. I point my weapon at the creature, yelling out a pathetic battle cry as the branch enters its mouth. It stops, nonplussed, then bites off the branch without effort. There's no way I can outrun this thing, and one-on-one combat will not have a good outcome. My only hope is that my body poisons the bastard. Then a shot rings out and the beast blinks. With the second shot, it falls on its forelegs and curls onto its side.

"You stupid?" the shooter says, running up to inspect the large, panting body. He has unkempt black hair and is wearing shorts with a ripped T-shirt, as if he'd been comfortable in his bed just moments before. "You go in the forest in the early morning? Never!"

"Yes, that was stupid," I reply. "Thank you."

He brings the butt of his rifle down against the animal's skull, which, given the size of the creature, shouldn't have had much effect, but the beast stops moving.

"What happens when you run out of ammunition?" I ask.

He doesn't answer. He takes out a knife and starts to carve.

So now what? I have no plan that'll get me home—not even a clue where I am to get home from. The rudimentary state of my knowledge is that if I travel east, I am in some way walking into the past; whereas a journey west is one towards the future. I'll pick the future since I now have a pretty shrewd idea of what the past holds.

25
Joad

My crude plan makes some critical assumptions. Foremost, I need to assume that this timeline is similar to my own in some important ways. Sure, the differences for me personally are monstrous, but the similarities seem more numerous. I need someone I had known since middle school to also exist in this timeline, to run the same business, and to be an old friend.

Thinking hard about the mirror problem and its implications for left and right turns, I direct Ria toward Red Mountain, and within half an hour we are driving up its slopes. Many of the vineyards I knew are now defunct, but a few are still operating, and in the moonlight I can make out the neat rows of dormant vines extending to the horizon. Mick Ito needs to still be in business, which is likely, because he'd never been the type to let the collapse of society affect his commercial aspirations. In fact, he's probably found a way to leverage it.

I'm relieved to make out the sign at the corner of an offroad from the main Red Mountain strip, which reads, right to left, *Bended Elbow Vineyards and Winery*. We turn up the road, and just as I'd remembered, Mick's small residence sits at the top, attached to the larger building that houses the tasting room and event hall. I take a deep breath in the hope that my luck holds out, and instruct the others to stay put as I get out of the car and walk towards the residence. Although I see no motion inside, warm light spills from the windows. I knock assertively. After a moment the door opens and standing in front of me is Mick. The bald head is new, but the boxer's nose and the scar above his eye are not. He stares at me with no sign of recognition.

"Mick—" I begin, and then his face cracks into a wide grin.

"Joad Bevan, you big asshole." He grabs my hand to shake it and then pulls me in for a hug. "It's been fucking years."

"It has. Hell of a long time."

"And out of the blue, here you are." I shrug. "You're looking good for an old guy. Last time I saw you, you worked for some super-secret outfit."

"No longer," I say. "I have some friends with me. Mind if we come in?"

Without answering, he waves towards the car and shouts out a welcome.

Inside, the decor is more Santa Fe than Red Mountain. One wall displays a large tapestry of southwestern design—vivid colors in geometric patterns. Painted on the opposite wall is a near life-size mural of a wrangler, lasso in hand and giving high-speed chase to a steer. A display stand houses a bronze bust of a heavily mustachioed man wearing a Stetson, a cigarette drooping from the corner of his mouth. And mounted in the middle of the dining room table is a vintage Winchester rifle that I remember giving him, although it had not been vintage when I had relieved the original owner of it. The others are looking bemused as they absorb their surroundings.

"Take the weight off before we do introductions," Mick says. "Beer or wine? May even have a drop of the single grain."

TIME WALL

"Mick, I need to get straight to it."

"That's Joadie for you," he says, grinning. "All business. Always was."

"Fact is, we're sort of on the run," I say. I feel guilty that I'm applying a battery to Mick's inner wiring, but that's what will get us to where we need to be the fastest.

His smile fades. "Who's after you?"

"The feds, I'm afraid."

"Yeah, okay. Upset someone at work?"

"Actually, yes."

"And you want to lay low here? No problem. I won't ask questions." He gestures towards a large metal safe with a combination lock in the corner. "That's where the firearms are." Someone whispers something but I don't look to see who.

"Yeah, thanks, Mick, but I'm not envisioning a shoot-out. We just need a safe place to work on a few things and then we'll be out of your hair. Is that good?"

Mick eyes his safe. "Good. Yeah."

We murmur our thanks.

"I'm afraid the house is small but the cave is big if you need space. We can set up whatever you want. And let's get your car out of sight."

"Really appreciate this."

"Hey, I owe you. You took the rap for me when I burned down the sports equipment shed." He grins. "No, wait, it was the other way round." He guffaws and slaps his knee. "You hungry? I'll rustle something up."

You sure about this? is what I'm getting from my colleagues' expressions.

After setting up work surfaces between the rows of five-story barrel racks that line the walls of the winery cave, we come to makeshift sleeping arrangements: Ria and Alfie have the spare bedroom and Mick is gallant enough to give up his own room to Gallie, leaving him and me to sleep on couches and reminisce, at least when I'm not feigning sleep.

Our immediate objective is for Ria to get a sufficient grasp of koson theory that we might devise a plan—one we're likely to survive—for rescuing… Gallie's husband. The likelihood of succeeding is something we don't talk about. Instead, we stay immersed in the physics, Alfie answering the barrage of questions we lob at her. I don't know why she's not sharing her identity with Ria. Less understandable than that is why the truth of it isn't obvious to Ria. Maybe the mother is half a head taller than the daughter, but otherwise they look to me like near-replicas. Or perhaps I only see it because I know.

This has gone on for three days and it's taking its toll on me. I'm exhausted, although none of the others seem to be winding down. Having recently lived the life of a professor in a small rural college, maybe I'm no longer fit for the relentless action I once knew. Even Gallie is bounding like a gazelle between discussions, and I watch her in jealous admiration.

Slumping on a couch, my eyes drooping and on the verge of sleep, I feel someone sit next to me.

"How you hanging in, Mirror Spouse?"

I sit up straight and rub my eyes. "I'm beat. Any progress down there?"

"They left me way behind in technical detail, so I thought I'd take a break."

I smile. "It's a bit weird, isn't it."

"Koson physics is the strangest—"

"No, not that."

"Oh," she whispers.

"You're Gallie and I'm Joad. It should be as simple as that, shouldn't it?"

She takes my hand without looking at me and I shiver. "It should be, but it's not, is it? The Joad I spent my life with is out there somewhere. He's alive, I hope to God anyway, and he's going through who knows what? You're Joad, I know that, but you're not him. It'd be all wrong." As she had always done, she easily read my thoughts, and I have a dozen points to make but I'm too tired to make them. Then she leans over and kisses me lightly on the cheek. I hold her shoulder, but then let go. What brings me joy gives her pain.

I muster a weak smile. "I understand, Gal. I won't make this harder for you," I say, getting to my feet slowly. "At least we can share a pot of tea like we used to."

"Alfie, c'mere." Ria doesn't take her eyes off the puterpad we'd borrowed from Mick as she drags up a chair for Alfie. "So, you used perturbative methods to come up with approximate solutions to the koson transportation equations, right? Methods only valid for small koson fluxes."

"Right," Alfie replies. "We wasted a lot of time trying to find an exact solution, but no cigar."

"I have an exact solution."

"What?" Alfie peers at Ria's screen.

"Yeah. That's it. Tried it out and it works. It also reproduces your perturbative solutions."

Alfie studies the screen for a few seconds. "Eeyah. Fuck me!"

Ria looks at Alfie as Gallie and I stand behind them to see the screen.

"That's it?" I say, but I get the sense that, at this point, any perspectives Gallie and I may have to offer are surplus to requirements.

"So, here's the interesting thing," Ria says. "You've interpreted all the transportation end points as being alternative timelines, which is true if the koson flux is fairly small. But if the flux is large, which you couldn't model with your perturbative approach, here's the transportation end point." Ria brings up a new screen.

"What's that?" Alfie and I ask in unison.

"I don't know, but it doesn't look like a regular timeline to me. It has the features of a kind of... a singularity."

We are all staring at the screen.

"You mean like a black hole?" I ask.

"No, no," Ria says. "All I mean is if the transporting koson flux is large, it's where you'd inevitably wind up. It's that kind of singularity."

"Okay, okay," Alfie says. "So if all some moron has are buckets of the right chemicals, but no theory, and no microflux control capability, and that's what they use to create a koson blast..."

"Then their victims would be sent to this place... a singularity."

"The fate of the Salkar camp," I say, "and—"

"And Joad."

Big discoveries answer a few questions but raise a lot more. Can our accelerators produce a sufficiently large koson blast to get someone to that singularity? We know they weren't designed for that. And a corollary question that dwarfs the importance of the first one: Would we be dumb enough to try it? The word *singularity*, although coined by Ria in the spur of the moment, does not generally describe any place you'd be excited to visit.

Alfie seems to have been distracted over the last day or so, leaving Ria to get on with the work. It's mid-morning on the fourth day of our winery stay when, passing the bathroom door, I hear something of a commotion behind it. Violent vomiting is my guess.

"You okay in there?" I ask.

"Yeah, I'm fine." It's Alfie, between heaves.

I join the others in the kitchen and see concerned faces.

"You guys been tapping the wine barrels?" Mick asks with a smirk. "Alfie said she's in the booze business, too, so she should know better."

"No," Gallie answers without humor.

Alfie finally emerges from the bathroom. "I'm fine, really. Just caught a bug maybe."

Gallie looks at me. "Both you and Joad."

She's right. I've been nauseous too, although I don't have it nearly so bad as Alfie.

Alfie picks up the cup of coffee waiting for her but puts it down again. "You know, I might try to get in another hour's sleep. Maybe that'll sort me out."

Gallie's eyes widen. "Wait a minute," she says, grabbing my hand to display my wedding band. "Oh shit. The Möbius inversion you went through."

I look around to see if anyone else is following this.

"The chirality—the left- or righthandedness—of all your amino-acid and protein molecules have been reversed. The amino acids in all living things have a left-handed chirality. But because you got flipped…"

"All ours are right-handed."

"So, when you eat proteins here, they do you no good because they're of the wrong chirality. They probably just pass right through you. I think you're both suffering from a severe protein deficiency."

"And where do we get our hands on the right kind of protein?" I ask.

"I don't think you do," Gallie replies. "Not here."

"Then me and Alfie are going to get a hell of a lot sicker, I'm guessing."

"You need to go home," Ria says. "And fast."

26
Alt-Joad

I sit opposite Sofia and Ayana as we tear strips of meat from primitive bones. As always, Sofia is too engaged in the solemn business of eating to join in our conversation. I'd been their guest for more than a week by now, and had fallen into a routine in which I paid my keep with a little manual labor. But now is the time for my announcement.

"I'm going to move on."

Ayana drops her food back onto her plate. "To where?"

"Whatever is west of here."

She nods slowly in a way that a teacher might who is about to explain to a naïve student why his idea is stupid. "What do you think you'll find there?"

"I really don't know, Ayana."

"You do know that trying to come back from a trip like that can be a problem." I glance at Sofia who has now taken an interest in our conversation, although without disrupting her eating pace.

"It's possible I'll find nothing out there, but if I stay here, then that's a certainty."

"Okay. I'll still ask you to consider it very carefully before you leave, Joad."

For a moment, I flatter myself that perhaps I'd be missed. I notice that Ayana and her sister are looking at each other as if coming to silent consensus on something.

"Wait there," Ayana says. Sofia studies me for a moment before getting back to her meal.

When Ayana returns she has someone with her. She gestures for the older man to sit with us. His eyes are fixed on me as he takes his place at the table. His head is shaved, his chin covered in gray stubble, and his bare forearms are tan and sinewy. I'd guess he's maybe sixty years old, perhaps older, and he's wearing clothing that is not typical for the camp. The body of his vibrant blue sweater is tight, but the short sleeves and hem are baggy. It's not a style I can place in any location or time I've visited.

"This is Rasul," Ayana says. She points to her plate but he shakes his head.

"Good to meet you," I say. "What do—?"

"Rasul is our brother," Ayana says. A career in time travel gives me an instant sense of where this conversation might be going. "And he's quite the explorer. He left us for his westward quest about three months ago. You'd just turned twenty-two at the time, right?" She looks at him, not concealing her sadness.

"Looks like you've lived a life elsewhere, Rasul," I say. He glances at his sisters, as if seeking permission.

"Yes, forty years." His voice is heavily accented but the English has a distinctly North American intonation.

"And then you came back."

"Missed us," Ayana says with a wry smile.

"I actually did," he says. "And my wife died. A wife of nearly forty years." This seems meant to take the smile off Ayana's face, and it works.

"Joad here is about to venture to the west," she says. "Any advice for him?"

He considers the question. "The palace. Is that what you're looking for?" I pause to make sure I'd heard him correctly.

"'The palace' did you say?"

He looks at his sisters as if surprised they hadn't mentioned the palace to me.

"There's a palace out there?"

He surveys me, checking that my surprise is genuine, but does not answer.

"I'm busy," he says, then rushes out of the cabin, slamming the door behind him. His sisters get back to eating, as if what had just happened was not strange, but I sense that this is not the time for explanations.

Later in the day, I help Ayana carry water in wooden pails from the river to the camp. I had already asked when I could talk to her brother again, but she had not answered. The notion of a palace is difficult to get out of your mind. The image I'd formed of it is probably ridiculous, so I needed to understand what he'd really seen.

"Rasul doesn't want to talk to you again," she says, lowering her pail to the ground.

"Why?"

She shrugs. "He's not well. Mentally, I mean. He doesn't talk much to anyone, not even me and Sofia."

"I just need—"

"No. I'm not going to let you interrogate him. He's fragile."

I put down my bucket and look along the river to the west.

"Is your story true?" she asks. This pivot puts me off balance, as I suspect was the intent. "Or were you sent here to find out what happened to us... what happened to your victims?"

"My victims? You're not my victims, Ayana."

She smiles. "Just thought I'd ask, Joad."

Ayana had invited me to visit their cabin, and when I arrive I'm greeted by the sight of a semi-automatic rifle and a canvas sack lying on the dining table, behind which Ayana is sitting, impassive and arms folded.

"If you're going, go now," she says. She gestures at the items on the table. "These are for you. In the bag are a few rounds and some food. After that runs out, you're on your own."

Now there's no mistaking that Ayana had wanted me to stay, to be part of her community and to live out my life with the Salkars. My next words are blurted out without consideration. "Do you want to come with me?" A smile flashes over her otherwise somber face.

"No, Joad. This is where I belong. My wanderlust is behind me. You know, I was on my international odyssey when my people were being rounded up like cattle and shunted over the mountains. There'll be no more of that for me. I'm going to be with them for whatever comes next."

I nod. "Will you say my goodbyes for me?"

"Just go, Joad, before someone sees I've given you one of our weapons."

I sling the rifle over my shoulder, pick up the sack, and walk out into the morning mist. I look west down the river and shiver, and then I begin to walk without looking back.

27
Joad

"Mind if we raid your fridge, Mick?" Gallie doesn't wait for an answer before emptying much of the refrigerator's content into a sack. We've decided to stick together if we're going to have any chance of finding my doppelgänger before being captured and locked up. Once the sack is brimming with the proteins Gallie and Ria will need, the four of us gather, standing as close as possible for the jump.

"Mick, if you were ever in debt to me, consider us even," I say.

"I was never in debt to you, asshole."

"Then I owe you one," I say as I raise my arm for Alfie to program my wrist accelerator. "Right now, you're about to see something unusual." I pull Gallie towards me and hug her close. Alfie does the same with Ria, and Mick's living room disappears.

We're in a copse of trees that I recognize. "We're following you," I tell Alfie as the tingling in my bones subsides. When we step out of the forest into Scalmere Village, I glance at Ria for her reaction.

She smiles. "This is where I grew up." Then she blinks a few times as if trying to clear her vision. "It's all backwards… like you said. Danke, Herr Dr. Möbius."

"You get used to it," I say. Ria seems to be taking it in her stride that, of all the places in the world, we have arrived in her hometown. These Bells are a strange breed. And then I notice something stranger still: the sign lettering looks wrong even to me. It seems that it doesn't take long for a brain to get acclimatized to mirror vision.

I take Gallie's hand. "Just be aware that it's you who's the freak in the looking glass here."

Alfie is standing alone and I can only guess her thoughts. Her mother is a short walk from here, if she hasn't been abducted by the DTS. Alfie starts to walk and we follow. We end up in a small café where we pack ourselves into a plastic-upholstered booth and order the most protein-rich offerings.

Once served, Alfie and I quickly dissect our sandwiches to extract the ham, then stuff it into our mouths to the bemusement of our server. We order more.

I offer to do some reconnaissance to make sure the Bells' home isn't surrounded by besuited goons, but with four of us sharing just two accelerators, we decide to stick together. Looking up the lane, I spot no SUVs and no one seems to be loitering. We walk towards the cottage in tight formation, alert to our surroundings. An old guy on his doorstep surveys us suspiciously as we pass, but then he recognizes Alfie and calls out a greeting. She waves back.

Alfie opens the gate and walks up the path, taking out her key. Nervously, she looks back at me, knowing that if her mother has been taken, then we'll have a real problem. I give her an encouraging smile, preparing for the accel if the wrong person answers the door. Alfie steps inside and we follow. The sitting room is still and quiet but for a ticking clock. Alfie calls out and it's met by silence. As Gallie is about to place a reassuring hand on Alfie's arm, a woman in a wheelchair appears from the kitchen. Alfie cries out something that's too thick in dialect to understand and rushes forward, throwing her arms around her mother. Ria slowly approaches them, watching the mother and daughter in their embrace. The woman in the chair looks up and takes Ria's hand. They look at each other impassively for a moment, then both smile.

"Mam, this is Ria," Alfie says, looking back and forth between them.

"I'm guessing you're the other founder of koson physics," Ria says softly. The mother looks at her daughter.

"My mam is—"

"I know who she is, Alfie. She's me. And I've known who you are for a while."

"Really?"

"Ha, of course. In part it was the Cumbrian accent." Ria smiles. "But it was mostly the way you think—how you see a problem, how you describe it, how you analyze it. You're wired just like I am, Alfie. Taught by someone exactly like me. But the clincher? When you were once excited by a solution we found, you said 'eeyah.' There's only one person in the world—any world—who used that expression. My father, your grandfather."

The three Bells smile at each other. I step forward and place my hand on Victoria's shoulder. "This is Gallie."

Alfie wipes a tear from her mother's cheek as she raises a shaky hand to Gallie.

I watch the Bells in conversation. All technical and none of it about them and their lives. Victoria's speech becomes fluent when the topic is quantum field theory and koson transportation. I notice an intriguing dynamic in which a certain glance from Victoria signals to her daughter that she is doing too much transmitting, too little receiving, and should shut up. And it works. It's a glance I would like to master.

I'm able to suspend the physics talk long enough to learn that Athol Green and his thugs had departed shortly after our escape, and they had been credulous enough to believe that Alfie's mother was no more than a sweet old lady whose daughter's work was a mystery to her. At least, that's the impression they gave, although I think it's only a matter of time before they show up again. Not even Green would be stupid enough to leave the cottage unsurveilled, which means our time here needs to be limited.

Sleeping arrangements are a little better than they had been on Red Mountain. Although I'm still relegated to a couch, at least I don't have the ordeal of listening to Mick reminisce endlessly. As I try to sleep, a hundred miscellanea dart about my mind competing for attention, worries bouncing back off the inside of my skull in case one might escape and lighten my burden. I eventually give up on sleep and consider going out for some night air, but that's too risky. Instead, I turn on a newscast. I haven't seen one in a while and have not missed seeing the unending chaos and misery. There would occasionally be a story about a timeline shift that someone claiming to be a tusker had witnessed, but my guess is that these people are generally cranks and charlatans. I let the newscast play while I go into the kitchen and help myself to a chicken leg, still catching up on my protein arrears.

... latest mass disappearances, bringing the total this week to eight. But this is the first recording of an event in the United States and...

It takes me a moment to digest these words, and I dash back into the living room.

This is footage from a camera mounted beneath a freeway overpass in the American city of Denver.

The blurry image displays a collection of makeshift tents with blankets strewn across the pavement, and maybe a couple dozen people lying on them with others gathered around a fire burning in a metal trash can. And then... they're gone—sheets, blankets, fire and all. The video is replayed.

This is a location used by a homeless community. Whatever happened here, it looks similar to the events recorded yesterday in Sub-Saharan Africa and Eastern Europe.

"It's happening here too." I'm startled and turn to see Alfie.

"Yeah. Inevitable, I guess. All it takes is for someone to find out what happens when you use the wrong accel isomer."

"Not just anyone though. Someone with a mission, it seems. I guess there are a lot of inconvenient communities in the world, and now there seems to be a solution."

Gallie had been exactly right. She'd tried to keep this discovery under wraps, tried to prevent a new chapter in the global chaos, but she'd had no chance of succeeding, impeded in this particular timeline by not actually existing. A tiredness descends upon me that has nothing to do with a protein deficit.

28
Alt-Joad

On the first day of my journey west, it was a practical paranoia that made me stop and crouch, heart in mouth, at every sound. But by the second day, these sounds didn't even cause me to break step as I knew I needed to make good progress, having estimated that there was maybe four days of food in my sack.

Another noticeable aspect of Day 2 was its duration—significantly more hours of daylight than the day before. This is a small victory in that it was something I'd predicted in an otherwise incomprehensible world. The idea that this place is hetero-temporal seems to be holding water, and, as I continue on west, the duration of day and night will each increase until I reach a point of near-perpetual light or dark. There, dilation would have accelerated surface time such that years could pass without the sun changing its position in the sky. So that's a forecast I'm now beginning to be confident about, at least if I'm remembering correctly what confidence feels like.

As for my destination, all I can claim is a palace. *A palace*. The absurdity doesn't escape me, although from Rasul's tale, coming across another community may be a more likely scenario. It doesn't take long to reach the point of perpetual daylight, and now I have only an internal and highly inaccurate clock to gauge time.

After a further day of travel there is still no sign of another community.

I wake up to the sound of screaming. It's loud and punctuated by a series of staccato hoots. I try to imagine what kind of animal would make such sounds, but then it becomes clear that whatever it is, there are more than one of them. I brush the leaves off me, cock my rifle, and army-crawl towards a tree. Sitting up against the trunk, I quickly peek around it. Fifty feet ahead, three figures are engaged in a heated dialog. The argument is consuming all their attention so I take a second, longer look. These are definitely not Homo sapiens, but their short arms and upright postures are not apelike either. Shallow foreheads, flat noses, receding chins, and bodies covered in a sparse fur, they must be some primitive species of hominin.

I wait, more intrigued than scared. Maybe once their conflict is resolved they'll be on their way, and I can be on mine. Then I hear rustling behind me and turn to see a fourth one staring right at me. I stand up slowly, smiling at it, careful not to bare my teeth, which my intuition tells me might be misread. It seems frozen at first but then looks around, maybe to check that I'm alone. Its eyes are wide and wild, and I can't tell if that's fear or a prelude to a frenzied attack. It's not holding a weapon of any kind and I have no sense of what an attack might involve, so I just maintain my feckless grin. Then it screams, waving its arms energetically before letting out three loud hoots and disappearing into the thick of the forest. The other three have gotten the message and are also hightailing it.

I wonder if I'm not the first Homo sapiens they've seen carrying a gun and once had a bad experience of it. That could mean there's a human community nearby. Or their prompt departure might just mean they've gone to get reinforcements. Either way, moving on rapidly while keeping my rifle cocked seems like the right thing to do.

Now and again, small mammals—some looking like rodents, others more like foxes—scurry across my path. This is comforting because it means when my food supply runs out I might have a chance of hunting down a meal, but it also worries me that I may be a meal for one of their larger cousins.

To the west, dark, heavily laden clouds swirl with almost comic rapidity, meaning the time dilation effect must extend well above the surface to at least the altitude of rain clouds, which, if memory serves, can be several miles. This is a very screwed up place and yet I seem to be acclimatizing. It's strange how you can get accustomed to shock, although I don't want to test the limits of that hypothesis.

From nowhere, Gallie and Casy make a sudden appearance in my thoughts. I had been fighting such thoughts since landing in this place, driven by the notion that the sooner I figure out where the hell I am, the sooner I can get home. But now that fight is lost as images and memories of my family flood in—their loud laughs, silly things they'd once said, jams they'd gotten into… I stop and breathe deeply. *No, not now.* The palace! Whatever in God's name the palace is, I'm going to believe it's my way home, and I won't give a moment's thought to how sane that belief is.

Then the downpour arrives on a strong gust of wind and I'm instantly drenched.

I take the last lump of meat from my sack and smell it. Descending to the river for water, I know I must be starkly visible. I scan around myself for any threats, then do a double take. At first it makes me smile. A few yards down the incline is what looks like a model village—a miniature town with little streets and buildings that you might see as an exhibit in a museum or a public park. It's about ten feet square and neatly enclosed by a little wooden fence, perhaps an inch high. I look around for any sign of the makers of this toy village. How dangerous could such hobbyists be?

But there's no one to be seen, so I take a step forward for a better look. The detail is impressive, even tiny trees and a lake. I can even detect motion in this toy town. I fall to my knees and rub my eyes to make sure it isn't just one of those damn floaters that have been accumulating in my aging eyeballs lately. No, what I'm seeing is people walking along streets, gathering in groups, entering and exiting buildings. So this could be where Joad Bevan is finally and convincingly losing it. My mind has just about clung on to sanity after a lifetime of dealing with the barking madness of time travel, of mutating timelines, of a lawless physics, and of a collapsing society, but these Lilliputians may be the final straw.

I crawl forward and it seems the village is a little larger than it had originally appeared. I stand up and take a step, and now the perimeter fence is a foot tall rather than the inch it had seemed before. I take a deep breath, steadying myself as I get closer, dizziness nearly overpowering me. The fence rises before me, and after a few more steps, it now towers over me. What had looked like matchsticks a few moments ago are now thick, sturdy poles, tightly packed and maybe twenty feet high.

It takes a second for me to set aside the obvious explanation of encroaching insanity and I resort to the possible physics of it. This world is not only hetero-temporal, it must also be hetero-spatial. That is, a one-foot ruler would be shorter at Location B than at Location A, but if you moved from Location A to B, you'd also be shorter so you'd measure yourself as the same height. That situation would be even beyond the wild imaginings of my post-doc research, but it's the closest thing I have to an explanation: The metrics of measurement are entirely dependent on location, for both time and space!

I hear something behind me. My heart races as I turn and look up at the colossus approaching me. I back away in pathetically small steps, but as he gets closer, he begins to shrink until he is standing in front of me at about my own height. He smiles, looking me up and down with curiosity. He is of weighty stock with a thick blond beard, and wearing a tunic similar to the one Rasul had worn—tight on the body and loose in the short sleeves.

"New arrival?" he asks. The language is English with no accent but an American intonation.

I stare and after a moment remember that he had asked a question. "Uh-huh, I am."

"From where?"

I don't know how to answer this on short notice, but he is not waiting for a reply, anyway.

"Come on then," he says, adjusting something between two of the fence poles that causes a small door to swing inward.

29
Alt-Joad

On the far side of the wooden fence is suburbia. Not only are there log cabins similar to the ones being built in the Salkar camp, but also single-story timber homes in a variety of designs. Villagers stroll along the narrow streets, all dressed in the couture of the once-giant. Two young women standing on the threshold of a house look at me, then seem to share their observations, which culminate in a giggle. The heavy-set man I'm following is too engaged in humming something loud and tuneless to focus on anything I'm saying.

"What's... Where are... How long has this place been here?" is the question I settle on pursuing while trying to narrow the distance his rapid pace has put between us.

"What? Oh, more than eighty years," he replies. "Where did you say you're from?"

I begin to answer but by now he's shouting greetings to someone as we turn the corner. Eighty years? I'm assuming that light, dark, and the position of the sun are not useful markers of time here, and that the concept of years was brought with them from elsewhere. We approach a structure much larger than the others; its gabled roof and log siding remind me of a national park lodge.

My host finally seems to have noticed that I'm not keeping up and he waves me forward with a smile as I follow him into the lodge. We pass under a flag fluttering in the breeze. A blue arc on a white background. The lobby area consists of benches lining the walls with portraits of smiling faces above them. My host is saying something into an open door, and then he thumbs me over to enter. The slight man inside has black hair, light brown skin, and an aquiline nose.

"Welcome to Underbridge," he says, getting up from behind his desk to shake my hand. "I'm Alsen Das, director of settlements liaison." Before I can respond, he points to the rifle slung over my shoulder. "That's a large weapon you're carrying. I don't think you'll be needing it here." He points to the corner and I take it I'm supposed to prop up my rifle there, so I do. "Just arrived? On world, I mean."

On world? I nod. "Couple of weeks ago."

"And where is your community from?" He's smiling at me in patient expectation.

"I didn't arrive with a community."

He seems perplexed. "Extraordinary."

I have no sense of what might be ordinary, so I nod in agreement. "And I'm from the United States of America."

He points to the slat wooden chair in front of his rudimentary box of a desk and we both sit. "Ha, okay. That's the origin of our community too. Mr....?"

"Joad Bevan. Where was your community before you arrived here?"

He stares for a moment, not so much observing me as taking the time to frame his answer. "Well, obviously, the history is unclear. But you'll find our communities have little interest in the pre-arrival period—both ours and yours."

"Communities? How many communities are there?"

"Oh, I really don't know. A large number, I assume, but I'm in communication with about a hundred." I feel my eyebrows arch involuntarily. "Hard to give a number—we like to merge villages. Deepens the gene pool," he says, smiling.

This is someone who seems not only able but also willing to answer questions, so I need to take advantage of that novelty. "You said 'on world.' What world is that?"

He seems to stifle a laugh. "Ah, well that's a question. I can tell you that it has little in common with our place of origin, but there are so few original transplants left, at least here in our community..." The sentence goes uncompleted.

"And you're the director of..."

"...settlements liaison, yes. It's my job to reach out to other communities, especially new arrivals. Help them settle in."

"And how—"

"Look, you're brimming with questions, and so you should be. But the best way is for you to see it."

"See what?"

"No, no. No more of this. Tomorrow, okay? First you need a good meal and some sleep."

I nod wearily and reach for my rifle.

"Would you mind leaving that here?" His schoolmasterly authority seems not to be argued with. "Rewa," he calls out and my humming escort returns.

Rewa's wife is a petite woman with golden curls, a retroussé nose, and an eternal smile. Their two small boys are too engaged in taunting each other to pay much attention to me. A small animal that, if not a dog then something close, is scurrying around us. The furnishings are simple but beautifully crafted, and Rewa is proud to tell me that he's the carpenter. As we sit down to eat, Rewa's wife asks me on which hand I wear my ring. My answer seems to dictate the bowl from which she will serve me, but I put this matter on hold—too strange to be a priority—and instead ask about the origins of Underbridge. I learn quickly that this is not a family with a keen interest in history. After dinner we play a card game I don't really understand, despite the exasperated attempts of the two boys to explain the rules to me. All strangely unstrange considering the circumstances, and I'm eventually given leave to go to my room, where there is a feather bed plucked straight from my fantasies.

I awake to a bright sun frozen in the sky and to the sound of the boys yelling, their mother yelling louder still to hush them. I roll over and what's looking back at me through the window is an ape—a colossal creature with bared teeth. My heart leaps as I spring from my bed, backing away from the window until I'm stopped by the wall. I look around me frantically, not sure what would be an apt weapon against this beast that dwarfs me.

But then the creature simply turns and walks away. Hell, this is no way to wake up, not before my sense of reason has kicked in. This was no King Kong but rather one of the hominins I had already met, now sufficiently far from the town boundary that its towering size had been a trick of the spatial dilation. I start to breathe again, holding my chest.

Before setting out for the day, Rewa proudly shows me the details of his longbow, which he'd crafted himself. It compares very favorably to any bow I'd seen across the centuries. We meet up with two other archers at the town gate: One looks like a leaner version of Rewa and the other is a slender woman with flowing caramel hair. Her pale gray eyes look me up and down like a zoo exhibit, but she gives no indication of whether she approves. Without introductions, we step out, and after a short walk, I glance back at the toy village behind us. Those first steps are dizzying, but it helps to just keep pace with the Underbridgers, who take it in their stride. We set off up the slope towards the tree line, then as we hike through the forest, Rewa takes the opportunity to catch up on his humming, while his thinner counterpart leads the group, the woman staring unabashedly at me the whole time.

The ambient light level seems to be increasing, which I take to mean the forest is thinning as we're approaching its far side. This make me anxious, not because of danger, but because the other side of the forest is something I haven't seen and it's likely to add a hundred new incomprehensibles to my list.

I cross the tree line and walk over to the leaner Rewa, who is silhouetted by a bright blue sky, peering over the edge of what may be a precipice. My host finally brings his humming to a conclusion and with a gesture indicates I should take a look at whatever is ahead of us. I take a breath and step forward. And there it is, laid out before me. It looks like a vast prairie framed by distant, snow-capped mountains and dotted with settlements interspersed by fields of crops and vegetation—golden, green, red, and violet. And there are paddocks containing animals that I can't make out from this distance. A river meanders across the plane, glittering in the sunlight as shadows of clouds drift across the landscape.

"Pretty, isn't it?" Rewa says.

I sit down before my shaky legs give way and scan the panorama. "How many settlements are down there?"

"You can count eighty-six from here." He points to the west end of the river. "There's a shrink zone over there like Underbridge: another thirty settlements you can't see until you get up close."

We sit quietly as I take in the view. Then I notice something in the far distance. Shimmering lights reminiscent of the aurora borealis—although they are randomly shifting around the full color spectrum—seem to be localized and originating from the surface. The source could be behind the mountains but it's hard to tell.

"What am I seeing?" I ask, pointing at the lights.

"The palace, you mean?"

I suck in a long breath. "And what is that?"

His look is one of incredulity. "What's the palace? I don't know what the palace is. No one does."

"So why do you call it that… the palace?"

He gives the impression of never having been asked that question before. "It's just the palace."

"And no one has gone to take a look?"

He shakes his head, maybe meant as a *no* or perhaps as a judgment on my idiocy.

The woman, who until now has not uttered a word, clears her throat. "Look how far west it is," she says with a crisp, no-nonsense diction. "You go there and you never come back."

Rewa reacts as if he has only now understood. She's right of course. If the temporal acceleration continues in the westward direction, an explorer could well return home in a very decrepit state. But for me, a man without a home, that disincentive seems slight.

"Can we go down there?" I ask.

Rewa shakes his head vigorously. "Mr. Das only asked us to take you here—to see the communities."

"You're free to do whatever you want," the woman says. "But only after we get you back to Underbridge intact."

Despite how little she says, I'm thinking that of all the Lilliputians I've met, this woman is the one I can relate to.

30
Joad

A sharp rap on the front door wakes me up, and Alfie sweeps past me to open it before I can get up from the couch to stop her. I hear her greet someone she must know, and I catch up with her in time to see her punching Mo Khara's shoulder. It's the Bells' engineer we had left behind in Paris.

"You're such an arse. Could your knock have been any scarier? It's lucky I saw you doing your strut up the path."

"Good to see you too," he replies with a grin, and then acknowledges me with a nod. When Ria emerges from the back room, Mo's double take verges on the comical.

"Yeah, you recognize her," Alfie says. "But that story can wait." Gallie appears and I gesture that everything's okay.

Alfie scans the lane outside before shutting the door. "What happened to you?"

"I have a question or two for you as well," Mo says. "Looks like you survived the koson blasts from my little contraptions."

Alfie's steely expression makes it clear that the next words out of his mouth better be an answer to her question.

He takes in the people gathered around him, who now include Victoria. As he looks alternately between Ria and Victoria, Alfie gives him a heavy tap on the shoulder to continue. "Green sent me here," he says, his eyes still on the two versions of Victoria.

I walk over to the window and pull back the curtain. There are no obvious signs of Green.

"He's not here," Mo says. "But he asked me to talk to you."

"About what?" Alfie asks.

"Wait," I say. "First, what have you told him?"

"He already knew a few things." Mo looks on edge, although it's hard to know if it's from fear of Green or Alfie. "They must have pulled apart the lab at the Crab. He knew we were working on koson theory and the technology. And they'd already seen the vanishing effects of using the wrong chemical isomer in the accelerator mix, so after your disappearing trick in Paris, even they could connect the dots. But they don't know what the hell we're up to; they just know we're up to something."

"And what details did you flesh out for him, Mo?" I ask.

"Not many. How could I? I'm just a dirt-under-the-fingernails engineer making a device." He turns to Victoria. "And I told them your mother knows nothing. That it's all about you, Alfie."

"You told them about inter-timeline transport theory?"

"Hell, no. As far as Green knows, we were just looking at the effect of moderating koson flux intensity. Kosons disappear you, and that's it. And that's all I really know too, by the way. Are you going to tell me what happened?"

"Not yet," I say. "You said Green sent you here. Why?"

Gallie tells Mo to sit down. I'm thinking that his unease is working in our favor, but Gallie usually knows better. He looks at Alfie for approval and she points impatiently to the couch.

"Green wants an amicable meeting with you," Mo says. "I guess he's worried you're armed to the teeth and might resort to something drastic. All he wants is to talk."

"I don't know this guy," Gallie says. "You trust him?" This takes me by surprise until I recall that the guy I'd slugged in a DC alleyway—the one who'd blasted my alter ego to God knows where—is not the Athol Green we're talking about. The worst I could accuse this Athol Green of is being an asshole. And who in the senior echelons of DTS was not? Yet, wouldn't the two versions of Green have a similar character? How the hell all of that works, I don't know. I shrug in reply to Gallie's question.

"So where does he want to talk?"

"A place of your choosing."

Alfie begins to say something but I stop her with a raised finger. "Okay. But just me. Everyone else stays right here. Any problems, like DTS showing their faces here, and all they'll find is an empty house and a stern wave of kosons. The Merry Crab at two o'clock will be a nice public place. Tell Green to come alone, otherwise—"

Mo nods. "Yeah, I get it. You know, for what it's worth, he seems like an okay guy to me."

"That right? And are you an okay guy, Mo?"

31
Alt-Joad

Even with the bizarre circumstances and unfathomable physics, I found Underbridge curiously dull, although a few days without excitement had been welcome. The citizens were anodyne, pleasant, and selfless to an extent that seemed to violate the laws of human nature. I'd have thought that some kind of competition for resources, or innate human foibles such as jealousy, or, to pick my favorite, irritation, would surface, but there had been no evidence of it. The nearest I'd seen was the incessant conflict between Rewa's sons. And even that more familiar dynamic was punctuated by unforced apologies and acts of kindness between the brothers. Yet isn't that a better life than one surrounded by driven and impatient assholes like me?

It's the day of my departure, and for the last time, I politely decline Mr. Das's plea to stay.

"Where will you go?" Das asks.

"The palace."

He smiles. "Ah, you're an explorer, Mr. Bevan. I will assume you understand the risks of westward travel."

"I do." This feels like the moment to try my luck. "Mr. Das, do you know what the palace is?"

"I do not, Mr. Bevan."

"I thought I'd ask."

"I often wonder," he continues, "if it has something to do with the messages we receive when a new community arrives. But perhaps I'm falsely connecting two mysteries in the hope of reducing our world of such mysteries by one." He laughs.

I nod towards my rifle for permission to take it from where it had been standing since first arriving in Underbridge. I'm realizing that this may have been the safest part of my journey.

Rewa escorts me to the gate. My rifle over my shoulder, I'm carrying the bag of supplies his wife had packed for me. I shake his hand and then he touches his forehead, which I take to mean *good luck*. As he opens the gate, I notice the archer I had met a few days earlier appear behind him.

"I'm coming with you," she says, brushing past me, a bow and quiver hanging from her shoulder. This does not have the intonation of a request or a question. It's merely factual. Rewa casts me a bewildered glance.

"Are you?" I ask.

She turns away and begins to walk, and I can only shrug before following her. I take the deep breaths necessary to avoid the queasiness of walking into a dilation transition. After a few steps, I look back at the miniature village and give a wave that is likely visible across the entire community. The woman with the flowing caramel hair is watching me impatiently.

"I assume the palace is your destination," she says.

I nod.

"Good. Mine also." She turns and walks on with an air that following her is optional.

I struggle to keep up as we ascend the forest slope, and consider the merits of trying to start a conversation that might slow her down a little. But there's something about the back of her head that discourages me. A journey that took more than an hour the previous time I'd made it lasts half that time, and I bend over to pant as I take in the view of the prairies, their scattered villages and fields of crops framed by the distant mountains. I look up at her in the hope that she'll be displaying sympathy rather than disgust for the struggling old guy, but it's neither, just indifferent observation.

"If we're taking this journey together," I say, "you're going to have to slow down."

"Downhill is easier."

It's becoming obvious why she wants to leave Underbridge. It had been a compassionate, considerate, and amicable community of which she'd had her fill.

"I don't know your name," I say, playing for a little rest time. She stares as if wondering why I'd made that observation. I suppose it hadn't been a question. "What's your name?"

"Kora."

"Okay. I knew a Kora. Corinth, fourth-century BCE. Been there?" Now I'm only amusing myself, maybe hoping she'll react better to confusion.

"How long are you going to need?"

I point forward for us to continue on. As we walk along the precipice edge, the glowing, colored ribbons of the palace appear more intense than I'd remembered, but then I'm distracted when I see the path that Kora is beginning to take. The footway, cut into the sheer cliff face overlooking the valley, is no more than two feet wide with a steep gradient and covered in rocky debris. "Is this the only way down?"

"Yes, why?"

"It looks... precarious." I sense she is not familiar with that word and has no interest in remedying that as she continues her descent. The small rocks beneath my feet rob me of any sense of balance, and when I launch some of them over the edge with my unsure steps, their landing is too distant to hear. But if this is where it all ends for me, it seems like a decent and honest way to go. Not by some incomprehensible timeline shift, or in a blast of exotic particles, but by slamming hard into the ground, old-school.

Yet Kora seems light-footed and oblivious to the hazard. She looks back occasionally to check that I'm still here, which for her, I take as an outpouring of compassion. It's when I'm beginning to get some confidence, feeling that my survival odds are better than even, that my foot slips. I cry out, lurching to shift my balance to the walled-side of the path, then I spread my hands, uselessly, onto the cliff face. Realizing I'm not in freefall, my nervous system catches up and my heart thuds hard against my ribs. Kora looks back up at me, her expression one more of curiosity than concern. She reminds me of a mountain goat that can balance on impossibly thin ledges, and lacks the imagination to understand that that may not be a universal skill.

As we reach the ground, I can finally breathe again—deep breaths that I had not dared take before. I look up, which causes me to stagger back from the sheer face. Kora has already set out without breaking her step.

32
Joad

I arrive early to scout the place out before Green arrives. The Crab's lounge is already beginning to fill and I take a seat with my beer, scanning the tables and bar for any sign of a DTS operative, although by now, I'm guessing the agency is savvy enough to avoid surveillance earpieces and black suits. My accelerator watch is in my pocket, my finger poised over the *Activate* icon which would, with the help of Alfie's programming, send me a decade back and a continent away.

One guy in a bright sweater and jeans has been looking me over for a little too long, so I return his stare, but then a young woman approaches him and he stands to kiss her. The pub is getting packed, so it seems business has not suffered due to Alfie's absence. I get up to buy a second pint and place it where I'll have Green sit.

He's on time and seemingly alone. Instead of the familiar expensive suit and bright tie, he's wearing a tweed jacket and corduroy pants, perhaps hoping to fit in with a look of the British landed gentry. I wave him over, but it takes him a while to spot me. Wending through the packed tables, he grins and nods a greeting before sitting down and taking a sip of his beer.

"That is nice," he says, sitting back in his chair. "It's been a while, Joad."

"Well, we'll always have Paris where you tried to arrest me at gunpoint."

Green takes another sip. "That was heavy-handed of me, I admit, and I've felt a little bad about it ever since. I just wish—"

"What do you want, Athol?"

He looks around, likely deciding that in this high-volume chatter it's safe to talk. "We need you. More precisely, we need Alfreda Bell."

"For what?"

He smiles as if to say he knows more than I think he does. "Dr. Bell's work has not been as isolated as you may think. For months, she was posting hints about it on the physics nets. I guess she couldn't help herself."

I'm too late to conceal my surprise. "What kind of hints?"

"No detail, but she'd been implying that she's extended tachyonics to include another class of particle."

"And...?"

"That's it. But something about the way she reported it made it sound credible to our people—not the usual crank crap. And we'd already observed the disappearing trick using the wrong tackychemical isomer, so... we put two and two together. Problem is, we had no way of finding her. That's where you came in, Joad."

"Did I?"

"Uh-huh. By sheer luck she contacted you."

"So I'd been under surveillance. Why?"

"Oh, come on, Joad, you're too modest. You're one of the most significant figures in the time travel industry. Did you think we were going to let you disappear into the night?"

Green looks up and I feel someone standing beside me. I lower my fingertip to the accelerator screen, but then I recognize her. The gray pixie-cut and turquoise highlights. It's the woman I'd spent the night with. I look at Green and he shrugs—not one of his.

"Hi," she says.

"Oh, hi…" *I don't know her fucking name.* There's an awkward silence and Green is clearly enjoying the moment. "This is…"

"You're busy," she says with a faint smile and walks away.

Green sips his beer, affecting to conceal his smirk.

I watch her walk away and then turn back to Green. "And now that you've found Alfreda Bell, what's your plan? Are you going to give her a research grant?"

His face becomes all business. "Because I want you to be honest with me, I'm going to be honest with you. You worked on the tachyon wall problem in your TMA days, right?"

Of course I did. Every TMA researcher, as well as others with less legitimate involvement in time travel, worked on the tachyon wall problem at some point in their career. And all with no success at uncovering why there's an apparent tachyon wall at the end of the twenty-first century. No tachyon transport, no time travel in either direction across the wall. Is it natural? Is it human-made? There are a lot of good questions and no credible answers.

"What has that to do with Alfie Bell?" I reply.

"It's a big concern, Joad," he continues. "The wall is fifty-one years away and no one understands a damn thing about it. In all the preceding millennia, there is no other such barrier. And now, here it is—unique across the history of time, and a mere half a century away."

Someone laughs loudly at a nearby table of youths getting an early start on their revelry. "Go on."

"Well, what is it? Is it the symptom of something cataclysmic? We've always assumed that it's just a barrier to time travel—maybe a good thing and nothing more consequential than that. We were too busy either traveling through time or trying to prevent it to spare any bandwidth for worrying about the wall. But what if it's more than just a barrier to time travel? What if it's a major spacetime phenomenon. If DTS doesn't try to understand it, prepare us for it, who will?"

"I still don't see—"

"We need the best minds on it, Joad, and quickly. And your friend Alfreda Bell is in a league of her own. We need her."

"You have minds in DTS already, don't you?"

"We have staff, Joad, not minds. You know as well as me that people outnumber real minds by a million to one. True creativity—"

"I get it, although I'm surprised that you do."

Green smirks. "You don't think much of me, do you, Joad?"

I shrug. "I hired you, and I don't hire people I don't think much of. But then creativity can eventually get replaced by mere pattern recognition. I suppose that's when we become fit only for management, and I can't say I'm entirely innocent of it myself." I sip my beer. "So what you want is a genius on your team. That it?"

He nods.

"Let me change topics on you, Athol. Why are you weaponizing kosons?"

Green's expression of dismay looks genuine. "What do you mean?"

"Vanishing camps set up by the homeless, refugees, that sort of thing."

"Why would you think DTS has something to do with that?"

"Because you could provide the technology to whichever agency is doing it."

"The effect of the isomer is known across the globe by now, and there are plenty of unsavories out there."

"Including us? It's happening in the US too."

"I tell you, I'm not involved in any of that. Nor is anyone in DTS I know of."

I lean back and fold my arms.

"Look, Joad, the world is on fire. You know that. Wouldn't surprise me if some asshole somewhere thinks they're serving the greater good by vanishing a few people. It's all part of the horrendous shit show we're living through. But what worries me is that we might look back on these as the halcyon days compared to whatever is on the other side of that tachyon wall."

I study Green's face and don't recognize the expression on it. Maybe it's what sincerity looks like on a face that has had little experience of it. I tip the remainder of my drink into my mouth and slam the glass down on the table. "Okay, I'll suggest a meeting with you. But just you, and I know you wouldn't be dumb enough to let me down. And I know Alfie pretty well by now. Fucking with her would be bad for you."

Green holds up his palms in a gesture of innocence.

I turn to see my bedfellow at the bar. "You'll have to excuse me now."

33
Joad

"So?" Alfie asks before I have a chance to shut the door behind me.

"The Crab is doing good business." No one is smiling. "Bottom line is he wants to meet you, Alfie."

"Why?" Ria is the first to ask.

"Well, it seems that Alfie's work was not as clandestine as we'd thought." Alfie and her mother exchange a glance. "Physics net postings got some attention."

All eyes are on Alfie. "Okay," she says, "in the early days I put a few things out there, but not much."

"How much?" Gallie asks.

"They knew someone had been developing a theory around a new class of particles," I say, "but they didn't know Alfie's name or location. Not until they tracked me here."

"And?" Ria says.

"Like almost everyone by now, they know about the disappearing effect of using the wrong chemical isomer, and they connected that to Alfie's well-publicized kosons."

"But they can't know about the inter-timeline transport," Alfie says, patting her thigh nervously. "I never posted any of that."

"No. Unless Mo told them. Where is he?"

"Told him to fuck off," Alfie says. "I don't need him in the mix for now." She chews her thumbnail. "Why does he want to meet me?"

I sit down, beginning to feel the effects of beer without food. "The tachyon wall problem."

There's an exchange of perplexed looks.

"What does that have—" Ria begins.

"Seems it's the big issue in DC. Makes some sense, I suppose. It's a mere fifty years out and no one knows what the hell it is. He claims they're worried that the tachyon wall is only the symptom and not the issue."

"Of…?"

"Of something big—a catastrophe of some sort. A spacetime cataclysm, I don't know." I look around me at the furrowed brows. "Gallie, in your timeline was this a concern?"

She shakes her head. "Not that was shared with me. But—"

"But it's not unreasonable, right? Inability to time travel trough the wall might be the least of our problems."

"Still not seeing why he wants to meet me," Alfie says.

"They need your brain on the team. He knows there aren't many like yours."

"There are none like mine," she states as simple fact. The two Victorias exchange a smile.

"Do you trust him, Joad?" Gallie asks.

I shrug. "My sense is that he's not the asshole that your Green is. Claims no knowledge of who's doing the vanishing trick on people… but I don't know."

Alfie shakes her arms to work off nervous energy. "There's no—"

"Stupid." It's a whisper from Alfie's mother, but it's enough to silence the room. She shakes her head slowly. "Why didn't we connect these things before?"

"What things, Mam?"

"The singularities." She points at Ria. "You identified the koson singularity—the endpoint of koson transport." She looks between Ria and Alfie as if asking whether she really needs to finish her point. Realization crosses both their faces.

"And the tachyon wall is a singularity by any definition," Ria says. All three look at me and Gallie as we try to catch up.

"You think the koson singularity and the tachyon wall are related?" I ask.

"Don't know how, but we sure as hell know that tachyons and kosons are related," Ria says as she and Alfie reach for puterpads.

The air is chilly but I'm warmed by bright sunlight on my face. Now that we have a détente with Green, Gallie and I feel comfortable sitting in the backyard of the Bells' cottage. Neither of us are deluding ourselves that we could do some good in the technical discussions happening inside, so we watch the sparrows visiting the feeder and the occasional squirrel popping out of the bushes to check what we're up to. Maybe once, I would have offered some value in that kind of technical environment, but creating new physics theory has little use for an aging brain. And as far as granting Green's request to meet Alfie, he'll just have to damn well wait until the time suits us, if ever.

"I had sex," I say. I hadn't planned to say it. After a moment of confusion, Gallie shakes her head and grins.

"Today?"

"No, when I first arrived in Scalmere."

"Okay." She watches the birds for a moment and then turns back to me. "You don't have to tell me that sort of thing you know. I'm not…"

"I know you're not. But… the thing is… and this is where you realize I'm crazy… I had been talking to

Gallie—my Gallie—long after the timeline shift that nixed her."

"And did she talk back?"

I nod. "Yes."

Gallie smiles. "I think I get that."

"You see, I'd asked her for permission to have sex."

"And did she give it?"

"She said it had been a long time since the timeline transition and that I shouldn't be such a wimp." Gallie smiles as she rubs her shoulders for warmth. We both look at the birds for a while, not knowing whose turn it is to speak.

"I hope you get your Joad back, Gallie. I do. But I can't see a hairbreadth's difference between you and my Gallie. Loving her is loving you."

There's a silence under which I feel crushed.

"Oh shit. No. Why did I say that? It's…"

She shakes her head. "No, it's okay. Other than the mirror-image thing, you're my Joad too."

My heart leaps. Had I heard it right? She'd called me *her Joad*. My impulse now is to hold her, to kiss her, to say to her what I've said to her a thousand times. But I steel myself for the brave words I know I need to speak. "The koson singularity is out there, I know it. And it's a place… a physical place… it's the place your Joad is waiting for you. And if anyone can figure out how we get us there and back safely, it's the Bells."

Gallie reaches for my hand. "Do you think the Bells are in the same league as Ram Prasad?"

I think the answer is *yes*, although it'd be heresy to say so. "They certainly outnumber him."

34
Alt-Joad

The pathway leading from the cliff face onto the prairies is little more than a foot-worn track through grasses and shrubs. Ahead of us is a fence enclosing a field that contains a smattering of grazing animals. The path curves to become parallel to the field boundary, and as we approach, what I'd thought to be cows I can now see are too large to be any breed I've seen. I don't ask Kora what they are, saving her limited tolerance of me for more critical questions. There's a community on the far side of the field, unfenced and with signs of motion on its periphery. The structures seem to be small huts, maybe teepees, but they are too distant for me to be sure. So this is another question that will have to go unanswered for now.

The aurora with its fluorescent ribbons of shifting hues is still visible from behind the mountain range, but this ground-level perspective gives me no new clues about what it might be. The next field we pass is covered in a blue-flowering crop. It may be flax, which makes sense as it might have a lot of uses here—fabric, soap, food, maybe. Or more likely, I'm entirely off the mark. I notice there is someone in the field surveying us from afar. Eventually he waves. It's obvious that Kora is not about to return the gesture so I do. That seems to satisfy him and he gets back to whatever he was doing.

We pass half a dozen villages varying in size and architectures. Some are comprised mainly of log cabins, others of thatched-roof cottages, some are obviously more mature with their two-story structures. About half the villages are fenced in, and some are producing thin plumes of smoke that hang high in the cool air, but we don't get close enough to any of them to make out their occupants. At one point, a family—two small children aboard a wagon being pulled by the parents—pass us traveling in the opposite direction, and the mother calls out a greeting in a language I don't recognize, but they have no intention of stopping for a chat.

The pace remains relentless, and after what seems like a solid twelve hours of walking, just when my sore ankles are about to give up, Kora takes an unexpected turn onto one of the many sidetracks we had been passing along our route. We now seem to be heading towards a village.

"Where are we going?"

"To eat and sleep."

"What's this place?" The structures, maybe yurts, are small and densely packed, and I can see plumes of smoke rising from parts of the village.

"I don't know," she says without turning.

"Then how do you know they're friendly?"

This causes her to glance back at me and I get the sense my question had been inane.

Can't be less friendly than you, I suppose is what I'm thinking. Two small bodies are scurrying towards us—children dressed in bright tunics, one red, one yellow, both giggling and calling out to us. Wanting us to follow, they lead us into the village where a group of adults in similar attire approaches us, laughing and waving, not even trying to communicate with us using spoken language. They have a Northeast Asian appearance, and they beckon us towards one of the yurts, out of which spill men, women, and children. The younger children rush forward and grab our sleeves. Kora brushes them off but I smile and hold their hands as I'm pulled towards the adults.

Without a word spoken, we settle around the roaring fire in front of the yurt where some kind of beast is being rotated on a spit. A beaker is thrust into my hand by a woman with wizened skin and a wide, toothless smile. She then raises her hand and presents her palm. After a moment of unsureness, I'm about to do the same when she lowers her hand and presents her other palm. Now I'm just staring at her stupidly as she alternates palms several times, her big smile never fading.

"She wants to know which type of meat," Kora says.

"Oh, how do I tell her anything's fine?" I say. "Anything's fine."

"No." Kora seems exasperated. "Which type of meat nourishes you?"

By now, I'm feeling quite comfortable being stupid, so I'm happy to just shrug. The woman taps my shoulder and shows me that she's putting two kinds of meat in my bowl, so I nod my gratitude. I sip from the beaker and cough as my breath is taken away. Everyone laughs uproariously, with even Kora compelled to flash a smile. Whatever I'm drinking seems to have reluctantly deviated from being pure ethanol.

The conversation around the fire is fast and entirely incomprehensible, but frequent, wide smiles from the villagers seem intended to make me feel included. Kora says nothing, and nor does she return a smile, but no one seems to notice.

After an hour of gorging and drinking, a teenage boy helps me to my feet. I'm escorted to a small tent in which I fall face-first onto an animal-skin rug. As I'm about to lose consciousness, the tent flap opens and Kora ducks in.

She asks, "Do you want sex?"

I ask her to repeat herself, but I had not misheard. I look at her and she stares back in earnest.

"Don't you want me?" she asks. The pause that follows is far too long for me to come out of this satisfied with my response. However, I realize that she is actually communicating with me and that's an opportunity I don't want to miss.

"Kora, will you tell me a few things?"

She seems nonplussed, as if by now we should be mounted and well underway. "What things?"

"Let's start with Underbridge. What do you know about its history? How it showed up on this world?" The Underbridge citizens had seemed reluctant to share the city's past with me on the grounds that it was unimportant, but Kora is no typical citizen.

She raises her eyebrows, as if resigned to the unsatisfactory direction this conversation is taking. "Underbridge just showed up here. Before that, I read it was a group of people on Uffern who had no homes. Lived under a bridge or something. May all be bullshit, but that's the story."

"Uffern?"

"That's where everyone comes from."

"Huh, okay. And what is this place we're in now? This whole world?"

"Nef, you mean?"

"All this is Nef? The rivers, forests, valley, mountains?"

She scrutinizes me for a moment and finally shrugs. "Yes."

"Okay." It's frustrating that she's finally loose enough to talk just when I'm too loose to frame a useful question. I lie back and close my eyes, sensing that I'm being surveyed for a sign of changing my mind about her offer, but that lasts only for the few seconds it takes me to pass out.

I wake up in the bright night to soft breathing. For an instant it's Gallie beside me and I begin to move towards her warmth, but when I open my eyes Kora is facing me, asleep and curled up with her hand under her cheek.

I have no path home. No way to find Gallie.

I rub my eyes in anticipation of a tear but they are dry. Maybe this palace has answers—answers that could get me home. It's unreasonable optimism to think so, but it's what I'll choose to believe. The palace at least gives me focus, meaning, hope. So what could cause those shifting ribbons of colored light? The aurora borealis is the closest phenomenon I can think of and that's caused by ionized solar particles shedding energy as they're accelerated in the earth's magnetic field. Might there be an ion source beyond the snow-capped mountains? And why do they call it a palace? Someone must have visited it at some time and brought back a story that spread, yet no one I've encountered claims to have met such a person. And it feels like all my comprehension of physics is redundant in this place, except for my superficial theories. Also, why are there so many primitive species here? I really have no comprehension of the very place in which I'm lying, so how could I even begin to speculate on the palace, a remote phenomenon on the far side of a distant mountain range?

I had been too distracted by thought to notice that I'm feeling quite nauseous. I hope the next community we visit is a little more sophisticated in its beverages. Maybe they will have heard of mixers. I turn over and Kora is awake, looking at me. *Shit.* This is a complication I hadn't anticipated.

35

My mother would have disapproved vehemently. Despite the shoddy way in which the TMA had treated her by curtailing a stellar career, she had been a devout adherent to the agency's principles and rules. Time travel for any purpose other than correcting egregious acts of mischief to the timeline had been strictly taboo as far as she was concerned. So she would certainly not have looked kindly on my little avocation—one that has now kept me informed and entertained for many years. I began my pastime in earnest long after the passing of my strong, beautiful mother, Victoria Bell, so she never suffered the shame of having such an ill-behaved daughter. The truth is I have been a tourist—a tourist not of places but of minds, using the technology of tachyonics to visit great scientists who shaped our understanding of the physical world.

Robert Oppenheimer had been one of them, and Ramesh Prasad, another: One the father of the nuclear weapon, the other of time travel. They were an interesting study in contrast. Unlike Prasad, Oppenheimer had not impressed me as a theoretician, but, my God, both men knew how to organize and inspire a team; how to motivate genius and achieve unprecedented outcomes. It seemed ironic that there had been such terror about the nuclear threat, yet such excitement about time travel. And which one of the two had ultimately wreaked more havoc, destroyed more hope, brought down civilization? Global chaos had been, in hindsight, an inevitable consequence of time travel—a world in which everyone knew that their lives and achievements could be undone in a capricious and instant shift of the timeline, in which the motivation to work, to love, to succeed, to live had all evaporated. And that was only the tip of the iceberg. Then there was the wall.

The motivation for understanding the tachyon wall had begun in such a banal place. If we can cross that wall, think of the marvels of technology that await us beyond it—technology to be brought home. *This had been the impetus for research into the nature of the wall, for surely such technology could bring great military advantage, or drive unimaginable commercial success, or realize some other puerile aspiration. The wall had been viewed as a mere inconvenience—a barrier that needed to be surmounted if the treasures of the future were to be plundered. For a long time, these ambitions blinded us all to some stark truths. Few at first had seemed to recognize that the wall could only be the effect of a profound physical phenomenon; one entirely unprecedented in time. And a profound physical phenomenon could only have profound consequences for something as frail and contingent as organic life.*

Another of my illicit trips was a visit to Albert Einstein—a young Einstein at his intellectual and creative peak. What a pleasure it was to talk with him, and what a frustration that I could reveal nothing of my own work. We talked of his universe of four dimensions, an idea that it seems had caused him more consternation than history had related. Why did time have such distinctive properties from the other three dimensions—up/down, left/right, forwards/backwards? He had struggled with this. With the help of his mathematician friends, he developed a robust understanding of spacetime as a four-dimensional entity, but he could not fathom why the human experience of that fourth dimension, time, was so different. For example, we sense that time flows inexorably, it passes, yet there is no such perception of the other three dimensions. All four dimensions are similar in their mathematical expression, so where does this experiential aspect of time come from? In that conversation, I had no idea how relevant his intellectual struggle was to the catastrophe that awaits on the far side of the tachyon wall.

Memoirs of Alfreda O. Bell
Personal Calendar: 79 years, 61 days

36
Joad

I can't tell whether the sound of smashing glass is inside or outside my head. But the yell is real, and as I leap up from the couch, shocked out of a deep sleep, Ria bursts out of the bedroom and points to Victoria's room. I bound over the back of the couch, shove open the bedroom door, and turn on the light. Alfie is kneeling over her mother who's lying on the floor. The bedroom window is shattered, although there's no sign of the projectile that caused it, and the curtain is fluttering in a cold breeze. There's shouting outside and I look out of the shattered window. Illuminated by gloomy streetlights are a dozen youths lobbing rocks at the cottages along the lane. One of them is kicking in a front door while others look on, laughing, but it's a laughter of fear more than mirth. Ria is still crouching by Alfie's side when Gallie walks in.

"What's happening?" she asks.

"My mam got up to see what was going on and she fell. I think she's banged her head." Alfie's eyes are wide with panic. "I can't tell if she's breathing. Mam?"

I touch the accelerator on my wrist. *Do we need to jump the hell out of here right now?* But this is not the time to coordinate a four-person, two-accelerator jump, so I run back into the living room and reach under the couch for the pistol I'd been carrying since we'd confiscated it from one of Green's men at the Crab. The threat of a firearm should be enough to fend off these kids, for now. At least, that's my calculation, which assumes they have no serious weapons of their own.

An unmuffled voice drifts up through the smashed window. "We're not going to hurt anyone if you just pony up what we want—money, valuable stuff. Okay?" He pauses. "We're coming in now so be cool about it." Then gunfire. The noise is continuous, like several weapons being discharged rapidly.

"Keep down," I shout above the din, which is now topped by the screaming from outside. I crawl into the bedroom, and by the time I reach the shattered window, there is silence but for Alfie pleading with her mother to wake up. I peek above the window frame and see a body heaped below. There's a small hole in the forehead of the kid who had probably just delivered the looters' message. In the lane, there are three men in row formation, reminding me of the Earp brothers at the OK Corral; they're arcing their pistols in search of missed targets. The road is strewn with bodies. Then a youth dashes out of a nearby cottage and starts down the lane, but a storm of steel follows him and he falls forward like a rag doll.

I look back to Gallie with her arms wrapped around Ria and Alfie. "Everyone okay?"

"No one hit," Gallie replies.

The silence outside is broken by someone calling my name. "You alright in there? Anyone hurt?" I recognize Athol Green's voice. "Can I come in?"

Gallie's eyes meet mine.

"Mam?" Alfie says, her voice breaking. "C'mon, Mam."

"Victoria needs help," Ria says. "Right away."

"The threat's been eliminated, Joad," Green calls out. "Can I come in?"

Gallie nods, so I open the front door. Athol Green is alone on the stoop, wearing a look of concern. Beyond him are motionless bodies on the ground but no sign of the gunmen.

"Were they armed?" I ask. He opens his palm, asking permission to enter and I stand back.

"It was only a matter of time before they showed up in this little burg," he says. "There are no safe havens, not anymore."

"Do you have authority to be shooting people?" My question does not seem to land.

"She's not breathing," Alfie says, appearing from the bedroom, her eyes sheeting with unshed tears.

Gallie is behind her. "We need to get her to a hospital, right now."

"Yes, of course." Green says. "Let's go."

37
Alt-Joad

I sit on an outcrop of rock, watching Kora aim her bow into the stream. She looses her arrow and then raises a fist in victory. The fish is wriggling on the arrow shaft as she wades towards the bank. By now we have reached the mountain foothills and the land is beginning to show some topography after a long trek across the flat prairies. Communities and farmed lands have become thinner on the ground, and it seems like several days—where I need to rely on sleep cycles to gauge time—since we'd passed a village. As I'd predicted, the villages seem more technologically sophisticated as we progress west, having benefited from the ever-accelerating passage of time. Yet these more advanced societies are interspersed with recent arrivals from Uffern that have simply been dropped onto the landscape.

The last community we'd visited had been by far the most technologically sophisticated. They had photovoltaic technology and electrical power; yet, as far as I could tell, no metals. In fact, I have seen no evidence of metals on Nef other than the scraps that had been plucked from Uffern along with their owners. The photovoltaic and electrical systems consisted of conducting organic materials, leading me to the unsettling conclusion that this state of technology was maybe further along than anything back home. But I could have all this wrong. While the primary language spoken there was recognizable as English, it had evolved in colloquialisms, pronunciations, and abbreviations to the point that I could pick up maybe half of what was being said. That, along with the laconic disposition of the citizens, had made it a frustrating experience. Kora must have felt quite at home. For her, each stop on our journey is all about food and sleep, and for someone who wanted to leave Underbridge to explore Nef, her intellectual curiosity seems slight. Or maybe I'd misinterpreted, and her motivation to leave had been more irritation than wanderlust.

As we'd gotten closer to the temporal zone of the palace, the shifting ribbons of multi-hued light had settled to a static shaft of violet rising vertically, and ultimately fading into the sky. Perhaps the multicolor effect from a distance had had something to do with the light's wavelength being perturbed as it passed through zones of temporal and spatial dilation, or maybe it had been some kind of fluorescence effect. The clouds above the light source are shifting so rapidly that they give the impression of snowy static rather than continuous motion. I interpret this to mean that the rate of time dilation is swiftly accelerating as we approach the palace.

So what are the implications of that? Are decades flying by at the palace as mere hours pass by here? Is it that severe? And then, how rapidly must time be passing here compared to that eastern location where I'd first been dumped? And the most painful question of all: How do any of these rates of time compare to home—to Uffern, to Earth, to my family? Is getting home even an idea worth contemplating? Kora thrusts a piece of cooked fish at me and I glance up at her, still lost in my own head. She waves the fish in my face and I take it. "Thanks."

"It's good," she says, sitting beside me on the rocks. We eat in silence—something I've become used to. I wonder idly if the dilation gradient could become so steep that if I were a few feet closer to the palace than Kora, could she watch me physically age in front of her? But this would make no sense because, from my perspective, I'd need to be standing still for a hell of a long time to provide that sort of entertainment.

"Do you think it's dangerous?" she asks, nodding towards the violet shaft of light.

Is this anxiety? That would be a brand-new emotion for my fellow traveler. Her irritability, impatience, incuriosity, and occasional sexual arousal have become familiar, but fear would be unprecedented.

"A radiation hazard?" I say, more to myself than to Kora. I'd wondered if the shifting colors might be due to the sort of high-energy charged particles that cause the aurora borealis, or maybe something akin to Cherenkov radiation, but the tight violet shaft of light we're now seeing seems less consistent with those theories. It's too coherent, too collimated to have a natural source, so if it is dangerous, it's deliberately so.

Until now, our journey has been surprisingly hazard-free considering the extreme weirdness of this place. Once, we'd spotted some kind of large beasts from a distance, but they'd shown no interest. I'm still carrying the rifle that Ayana had given me, but I've not discharged a single shot—not even taken aim. In contrast, Kora's expert use of her bow is what has kept us fed since we left the last community. Small animals, some recognizable, some not, have crossed our path and Kora has taken her pick, never missing her shot. And she would have had no difficulty getting into the Scouts with her fire-making skills. If she had not shoved past me at the Underbridge gate and announced that I would not be traveling alone, this would have been a very different trip.

She doesn't elaborate on what dangers she's thinking about, but since this is a full-throttle conversation by her standards, I try to take advantage of it. "Can I ask you something? I notice that no one in any of the communities we've visited wants to talk about their origins. About… Uffern."

Kora spits out a fish bone. "Why would they?"

"Seems—"

"It was hell as far as I've been told. In some villages they don't even call it Uffern, they call it Hell."

"Really?"

She shrugs. "The whole place was burning down." She picks a bone off her tongue and flicks it away. "Don't care about history. Not interested."

I feign surprise. It occurs to me that the people of this world don't see themselves as victims, but more as the beneficiaries of a deliverance. Yet, for those doing the delivering, I'm sure the motivation had been annihilation, plain and simple. I'm too slow coming up with my next question as, by now, Kora is walking down to the stream to clean off her arrow.

I pick up my bag and rifle and study the slopes of the foothills. The base of the violet shaft seems like a reasonable place to target. Maybe what I'm seeing is in fact ionizing radiation and we'll collapse from exposure to it before we get there. But the way I see it, what do I have to lose? My wife? My family? My life? They're gone, so for me the stakes are low. But then Kora needs to make her own decision when the time comes.

She approaches me as we're about to set out. "Do you like me?" she asks. Her expression is entirely guileless.

I smile at her. "Yes." And only after I'd said it do I realize that it's true. She turns and walks on.

38
Joad

Ria wraps her arm around Alfie as they come out of the examination room. Alfie is shaking, her cheeks stained with tears. Gallie steps forward to hold Alfie and Ria joins me.

"They said she probably died the instant her head hit the table," Ria whispers.

"You okay?" I ask her.

"You're thinking it might be strange to see yourself dead?" she asks. "She wasn't me. It never felt like she was. No more than Alfie feels like my daughter."

I watch as Gallie comforts Alfie, and I know that I don't feel the same way. That's *my Gallie*.

The waiting room doors opens and Athol Green enters, taking in the scene and smiling sympathetically, but at no one in particular. He'd been good on his word and acceled us immediately to a hospital in Washington, DC, yet I still don't sense a single quark of sincerity in his entire body. His smile seems like an affront to our grief.

"I want to make sure you're all safe," he says. "We have a hotel close to the DTS that has been completely secured and I have four rooms waiting for you, if you want them." Instinctively, I wrap my hand around my watch accelerator, wondering what the difference might be between a secure hotel and a prison.

"Thank you, Dr. Green," Gallie says. "Alfie shouldn't be alone. Ria, would you mind sharing a room with her?" Ria smiles and nods. "And Joad and I can share."

I fight to conceal the tsunami of emotion that just hit me, but I nod somberly, noticing Green's expression of curiosity.

"Of course," he says.

It's interesting that he doesn't seem to recognize Gallie. I would have thought that a senior DTS officer would be a tusker, taking all the right serums. But if that were true, he would remember Gallie from before the timeline shift that had taken her away from me.

He pulls me aside. "I'm sorry about what happened, Joad. I'm just glad none of you were hurt."

"Were those kids armed? They weren't, were they?"

"We didn't know. Should we have waited to find out? And to be frank, rioters coming to a sticky end is a good message to get out, don't you think?"

"So you'd shoot down half the world's population? Is that the message? Or maybe you can just annihilate them with your newfound death ray?"

He smirks. "I've already answered that question. I have nothing to do with any of the disappearances and neither does anyone I know in DC." He notices my accelerator. "Do you want to keep that? We could recharge it for you."

I smile wearily. "I'll let you know, Athol, thanks." With that thought, I glance at Alfie. Her watch accelerator is gone. *Shit.* "Kind of you to offer."

"Anytime, let me know," he says, now turning his attention to Alfie. "Poor thing. I am hoping we can get her on our team as soon as possible. I know she's in distress but work can be a good distraction. Tell me when you think the time is right." He walks over to Alfie and Gallie. "So sorry for your loss, Alfreda. Let me know is there's anything I can do."

With that he exits the waiting room and Gallie and I are left looking at each other. *Asshole*.

I close the bedroom door behind me. "Why—" I begin.

Gallie shakes her head, steps forward, and kisses me lightly on the lips. I caress her cheek and kiss her back. As her arms wrap around my waist I feel her warmth against me. My sense memory leaps to the first time we'd made love—in the woods of colonial America. My heart is racing just as it had then. But this time there's something new in the stream of emotions that is coursing through me, and I realize that it's fear. What if I do something that makes her remember I'm not her Joad, that I'm an imposter, a poor replica? She takes my hand, leads me to the bed, and we fall onto it. The fears evaporate. This is Gallie and Joad together. It's that simple, that natural. It's something that always had to be.

Gallie opens her eyes and turns toward me. "Were you looking at me?" she asks.

"I was. I am."

She smiles. "That's okay. I was looking at you earlier."

I remove a strand of tousled hair from her eyes. "Is it still weird that I'm… the left-to-right thing?"

"Like you said, it's me who's back-to-front here."

"I could put my wedding ring on the other hand if it helps," I say, stroking her hair. "But that does raise a good point. We need to get you and Ria some of the right proteins."

Gallie grins, putting her palm on my chest. "So romantic."

39
Alt-Joad

By now we are only a few hundred feet below the snow line and the air is crisp. Our route to the palace is becoming less direct as we wend through the rocky outcrops of the mountain foothills, trying to avoid the challenge of a direct climb. But still, the ascent is becoming steep enough for me to need a panting break every few minutes. Even though we seem to be close to the shaft of violet light we've been calling the palace, the rapid cloud motion above it indicates that the time dilation gradient is getting ever steeper. But I've given up trying to guess the safety implications of this, figuring that provided the dilation between the tip of my nose and the back of my rear remains small, then my body should remain intact.

We reach a small plateau covered in grasses and buttercups beyond which is what looks like the final ascent to the source of the beam. This is a good place to get some sleep before the exertion of the final leg. My mind shifts from the possible hazards of the violet beam to the opposite risk: the one of an anticlimax, of disappointment. What if there's nothing to see and the beam simply fades like the end of a rainbow? That'd be the more devastating scenario because I'd be halfway up a mountain left with the question of *now what?* Maybe we could go back to Underbridge or another of the communities we'd visited. What would that life look like? It'd be one without Gallie and without Casy for sure, but I'm resigned to the fact that that'd be true of any outcome. Even in the unlikely event that the palace is actually a physical place as wondrous as Oz, it couldn't return to me the things I'd lost.

Kora has had the same thought about resting here, and she throws her quiver to the ground, unlooping the bow from her back. We're breathing out vapor and I can tell that this will be a chilly slumber. At least we're unlikely to get any colder in this world of perpetual daylight. I collapse forward onto my groundsheet and relish the relief in my suffering ankles.

As my muscles uncoil, I look up the slope towards the beam, no longer in scientific speculation but in admiration of its simple beauty. After a while, I begin to shiver. Pulling the groundsheet around myself, I shift onto my side, realizing that sleep might turn out to be a lost cause. Kora is also shivering and staring wide-eyed into the sky.

"Hey," I whisper. "Cold?"

"Freezing," she replies, also in an unnecessary whisper.

The idea I have is okay because it's about survival. "Want to huddle for warmth?" I ask.

She drags over her groundsheet until it overlaps with mine. Then she looks at me as if to ask how this will work.

"It's called spooning," I explain. "To minimize our exposure to the elements." She seems familiar with the concept and lies beside me before turning on her side and shuffling backwards. I notice that her hair smells of fresh air as I remove it from my face. Then I wrap my arm around her and pull her closer. *Effective heat transfer.* She entangles her icy feet with mine, which seems in the spirit of our plan. As we lie still, I feel the rise and fall of her warm body. This seems to be working although I'm no closer to sleep. Then she moves—just a small wriggle of her hips, no more. *Damn, is that all it took?* There's no way to conceal my reaction—not in this position, at this proximity. She turns her head, her eyes straining to see me. I hesitate, then hold her chin gently with my fingertips. Then I kiss her.

I smell the food before my eyes open. Kora must be cooking the small mammal she had hunted the day before. I raise myself up on my elbows and immediately reach a firm decision. Not a word must be spoken about last night. Not about any of the three encounters I'm now remembering.

"I'm sorry," I say.

"About what?" she asks, looking up briefly from the rotating animal.

Well, yes. About what? Kora isn't the one I should be apologizing to. It's someone else—someone who may be a million miles and ten millennia away.

After breakfast I begin to pack my groundsheet.

"Not yet," she says, pushing me down to the ground.

The beam is close, seeming to originate no more than a hundred feet up the slope. I'm getting the impression that it narrows towards the ground, as if it originates at a vertex, although that's impossible to verify because the base of the beam is behind an outcrop of rock. Cloud motion above no longer seems accelerated, which means we must be in the time dilation zone of the beam itself. There's no sign of structures or people, and the landscape appears no different here except for the light dusting of white flakes as we approach the snow line. I'm not feeling the sickness that would accompany exposure to ionizing radiation, so the odds are that the disappointment scenario is the one that's going to play out. Why the hell would they call this the palace? It's now seeming likely that it had only ever been seen from a distance, where the ribbons of shifting colors had given it a look of mystery and grandeur.

Kora has also stopped to scan the terrain. Pins of sunlight reflect off the distant communities dotting the prairie, and it's beginning to look like one of those villages will turn out to be my fate.

I continue the ascent. The rock lying between me and the source of the beam is now only a few feet away and it's clear that the light shaft does taper, transforming at its base from a cylinder to a cone. I climb the rock and look down at the terrain ahead. My heart slumps into my stomach and the cold hits me hard. There is nothing new in what I'm seeing except that the shaft narrows to a sharp vertex where it touches the ground. I jump from the rock and take a few steps toward it until I'm directly beneath the cylinder of light. It takes me a moment to register that Kora has been saying my name, so I turn. *Fuck!* I stagger backwards, struggling to keep my balance. She is giant. For a few moments I'm shocked, but then the logic of it falls into place. I've walked into an area of spatial dilation.

"It's like Underbridge," she says down to me and then approaches, shrinking into my little patch of space. "The palace may be right here, but small."

I look back to where the vertex of light touches the surface but see no structures beneath it. This is not like Underbridge where a seemingly miniature village was visible. But what if the spatial dilation here is far more severe? I pick up a pebble and toss it at the vertex, watching it vanish shortly after leaving my hand.

"I think you're right, Kora."

I'm about to ask her if we should risk going on, but she is already sweeping past me towards the vertex, and she is shrinking as I jump forward to grab her hand. "Together. We stick together, okay?"

She nods as she drags me into the light.

40
Joad

Alfie agreed to work with DTS, for now. But because the notion of becoming their employee was just too repulsive to her, her contributions would be *gratis*. While staying in the hotel Green had provided, we kept to the rule that the four of us had agreed to: there would be no conversations about koson theory and timeline travel since our rooms were likely bugged. That must have been frustrating for the Bells, especially since it would have been a welcome distraction for Alfie, who had become very quiet since her mother's accident. Gallie and I had occasionally plucked up the courage to look out our hotel window, where it was now clear that DC could no longer maintain the pretense of being above the chaos. We'd see the spontaneous formation of rabbles, cars being set alight on the mall, and rocks being hurled at any official-looking vehicles. Occasionally, the military would show up in force and things would settle down quickly, albeit temporarily. The four of us spent time in each other's rooms, mainly to make sure that Alfie was coping.

We now had a single wrist accelerator between the four of us, Green's people having removed Alfie's device when she'd been too distraught to care, which reduced our options. Fitting four people in a single tachyon/koson blast radius would be a challenge and risk leaving someone's extremities behind. Furthermore, the tackychemical charge was getting low, notwithstanding the fact that this clever little device uses only microquantities of the chemicals per accel.

I took a trip alone to a small grocery store in Scalmere, to scavenge the right proteins. Alfie was able to tell with a few readings from the accelerator that the hotel had been placed inside a tachyon shield, obviously to curtail any unwanted travel in or out. However, tachyon shields do nothing to prevent koson transport, and this allowed me to take a crucial trip. It had been a nerve-racking ordeal because, had anything gone wrong, I'd have been stranded in another timeline. But Alfie assured me that her programming of the device was accurate and that there was enough chemical charge to get me there and back.

I acquired a stash of cooked meats—not the Bells' Scalmere, but the inverted one with all the right proteins. That seemed like the place I'd be least likely to encounter problems, and my guilt at charging out of the store with food I couldn't pay for was more than offset by the relief of arriving back at the correct location. We stuffed the small room fridge to capacity while Gallie and Ria immediately ate anything that wouldn't fit.

The knock on the door is on time, and I open it to Athol Green's feckless smile. "I'm coming with Alfie," I say before he can launch into his insincere pleasantries.

"There's no need—"

"I need to be with her at first. I know you understand." He looks over my shoulder and I assume from his reaction that Alfie has nodded decisively. This is not the time to let Green waft her away.

The drive up Independence Avenue is a short one. I try to get Alfie's attention, although all I plan to do is smile reassuringly, but she's motionless, looking out the window of our heavily armored limo. We pull up in front of the DTS headquarters, and, surrounded by Green's security detail, we ascend the steps to the main entrance, get our visitor credentials, and are led to the elevator, which is open and waiting. It seems like a lifetime ago I'd walked into this building to be fired by Green. We arrive at the basement level and the doors open to a congregation of people I don't recognize. A short, skinny man with a thin thatch of brownish-blond hair is simpering as he grabs Alfie's hand.

"This is a real pleasure," he says. Alfie looks at me as if her worst fears are already being realized.

"Let's leave them to it, Joad," Green says. "This'll all be above our heads. I'll buy you breakfast."

Alfie nods.

The DTS cafeteria is a large open space that used to be flooded with daylight through large plate-glass windows, but now the protective metal screens give it a lugubrious atmosphere. I sip the coffee Green bought me but push away the donut.

"Thanks for helping make this work, Joad," he says. "Alfreda's going to be a critical asset for us."

"She's bright," I say. We smile at this understatement.

"I think—" Green begins just as his phone chimes. He raises a finger for me to stand by and answers the call. "Shit!" he says and hangs up. "Sorry, Joad, gotta go—more upstairs bullshit. Just settle in here and I'll be right back." His irritation seems genuine, likely because his primary job for the day had been to stick with me and keep my nose out of their business.

I'm finishing my coffee and reaching for the donut when I notice a guy a few tables away staring at me. He has the expression that he's almost but not quite sure he knows me.

He's bearded and wearing a pressed white shirt, dark tie, and bright green baseball cap. That could only be… I struggle for the name. Tommy Galanis. I grin and with that he walks over.

"Tommy!" I knew him from my days at TMA but have not seen him in years.

"Look at you, you young bastard. You're like Dorian Gray," he says with a wide, yellow-toothed smile as he shakes my hand vigorously.

"And you're like his portrait," I reply, laughing. "Sit down. I didn't know you worked for DTS."

"Yeah, held my nose and made the jump. You too?"

"Nah, just visiting—you know Athol Green, right?"

He raises his eyebrows. "Green! Then you're on board?"

"No, a DTS life is not for me, Tommy."

"Not that," he says and then looks at me, waiting for me to understand.

I maintain my smile. "So catch me up. What's your job here?"

He's eager to tell me, and we chat for a while, comparing the misery of a DTS life with that of teaching in a small midwestern college. Once our conversation has some momentum, I return to something he had said earlier. "You asked if I was on board."

His smile fades. "Yeah, I meant…"

I grin to maintain the spirit of banter, hoping that this will not be the moment he abandons his legendary indiscretion.

He looks around us and then leans in. "You need to be part of this, Joad. You of all people. I just assumed that if you're talking to Green…"

"He hasn't raised it yet—had to run off and put out some fire, but I was wondering what all this was about."

Tommy seems to be weighing the pros and cons of anticipating Green's conversation with me. "Okay, so you'll hear about it an hour earlier. So what?" He leans in further. "It's the Ark Project." I furrow my brows. "You know the panic-du-jour is about the tachyon wall, right? Big fucking mystery, of course, and now the conventional wisdom is that it'll be a bit of an apocalypse. So the Ark is the escape plan. For some of us, anyway." He grins.

"What do you mean *bit of an apocalypse?*"

"You know. Well, no one knows. But the working assumption is that there's nothing good on the far side of the wall. Armageddon and all that."

"And the... the Ark Project?"

"It's the tachyon ride that gets us out of here before we hit the death wall. In fact, back to your old haunt—Tomatotown."

I hear myself take in a sharp breath.

"How long did you run that place, Joad? Really makes sense that you're in on the Ark."

I sit back in my chair and affect nonchalance. "So we're saving the lucky few by sending them back ten millennia to the TMA research campus I once managed?" I smile and shake my head.

"No need for that setup once we took down the TMA shingle, so it's a good use of resources, right?"

"Right. And what exactly is the Ark Project?"

"You know, setting up supply chains, logistics and all that. We have millennia of resources to draw on. A clever plan, no?"

"Wow, Tommy. Well, I'll be sure to act surprised when Green tells me all about it."

"Yeah, you should. Green is quite the powerhouse nowadays. He seems to have even more sway than the secretary. You probably know he heads up the two big DTS programs: the wall research plus weapons."

"Koson weapons?"

Tommy nods. Then we share a few more anecdotes from back in the day. "Be sure not to mention me" are his parting words.

41
Joad

I meet up with Alfie in the DTS lobby at the end of the day. She's shaking hands with the short, skinny man who looks like he may have maintained his obsequious grin throughout the entire day. Her expression is neutral, giving no clues about how she had fared. He starts to say something to her but she has already begun to walk away. In the limo she sits back in her seat and folds her arms.

"How you hanging in?" I ask.

She shrugs. "Fine." But this is not what *fine* looks like for Alfie. Some kind of dismissive wisecrack would have been more welcome, and I give her hand a pat.

"This place—" she begins, but I put my finger to my lip. I'm suspecting the vehicle is heavily wired, and if not, the driver is unlikely to be a professional chauffeur. Alfie stares out the window as we take our short ride, but the tinted glass prevents the scowling pedestrians from seeing in. I try to imagine the thoughts behind those scowls. *Look at those bastards in a limo, insulated from all the chaos.* And maybe they're convinced that before a timeline switch, they were the ones in the limos. Of course such thoughts are irrational, but I get it, and I count it a good afternoon when that disgruntlement has not erupted into violence. I notice the chauffeur is observing us in his mirror and I give him a friendly nod.

Our only safe place to talk is the hotel restaurant. It lies at the center of a ten-story hall, lined with the balcony corridors. At meal times, the cacophony of diners along with the muffled acoustics of the cavernous space make it impossible to overhear what's being said, even at the next table. The four of us wait for the waiter to leave and then lean in.

"How was your first day?" Gallie asks.

Alfie shrugs. "Straight into technical discussions."

"About?"

"The tachyon wall."

"No talk of koson theory?" Ria asks.

"No," Alfie says. "Biding their time."

"Where are they on understanding the wall?" I ask.

"They're nowhere based on what I heard," Alfie replies. "I mean, if the best and brightest in TMA couldn't make a dent on it, then what are these people going to do? They're just going through the motions."

"I think you're right," I say. "So I had a useful conversation today once Green was out of the way. Gallie—you remember a guy called Tommy Galanis? Did he show up in your version of things?" Gallie's nod is noncommittal. "It seems they're convinced the wall is a symptom of some kind of cataclysm, and they're developing an escape project."

Everyone at the table starts in with their question, which is likely the same one, but they let Gallie proceed. "Escape to where?"

"Back. Back up the timeline," Ria answers for me. "Where else could it be?"

I nod. "Specifically, about ten thousand years back."

It takes Gallie a moment. "Tomatotown?"

I snigger. "That's the place. The real estate is already developed and the site was abandoned."

Alfie looks back and forth between us. "Is someone going to explain? Tomatotown?"

"TMA Temporal Operations—TMATO. Siting it in the deep past kept it nice and safe, at least for a while," I say.

"And Joad was its director," Gallie adds.

Alfie arches her eyebrows and shakes her head. "Another loop my mother was not in." She looks at Ria who is idly rotating her glass on the table.

We pause as the waiter returns and presents a bottle of wine. "It's fine, you can just pour it," I say. We wait until he leaves.

Ria shakes her head. "What a massive helping of shit."

"You thinking of anything in particular?" I ask.

"Absolutely everything. We're in freefall. We've got bastards using koson technology to annihilate entire populations, we've got DTS assholes and probably other elites developing cozy estates in the deep past to rescue themselves from an oncoming apocalypse, and meanwhile the world burns."

"And it's just a matter of time before word gets out about what's coming our way," Alfie says, "and that'll raise the fucking chaos to the next level, so the shit we're in will only get deeper."

"One correction," I say. "We don't know that the kosons are annihilating anyone. They didn't annihilate us and the singularity could well be a real, physical place, just like the other timelines."

Alfie scoffs "Yeah, well, if that's what it takes to give her hope," casting a savage glance at Gallie. "But you have a new Joad to fuck now, don't you? So relax." Alfie stares at me defiantly before looking down and fondling her knife. There's a silence during which I avoid Gallie's eyes.

"So let's forget the DTS team, Alfie," I say. "Do you think you could make progress on the tachyon wall?"

She shakes her head without looking up. "My mam had some ideas about connecting the tachyon wall with the koson singularity, but I don't know how to push that forward without her. We worked together—we were in each others heads, and nothing works without her." Alfie wipes her eyes. "She always knew what I needed, when I should come up for air. She'd tell me to take half a day to do something whimsical, so we'd watch a stupid movie or play a game. And she was always right. It was always what I'd needed." A smile flashes across her face. "She said that after teaching me real physics, her second mission in life was to give her daughter a sense of whimsy. I'm afraid she failed there."

"I'm so sorry, Alfie," Gallie whispers. "Maybe Ria—"

"Ria is not my fucking mother. She's a sad imitation. Just because she's a lot smarter than you doesn't make her smart enough."

We sit quietly, no one willing to risk the wrong words.

"I'm tired," Alfie says after a long silence and pushes back her chair. "I'm going to bed." She walks away and Gallie stands to follow her.

"No," Ria says. "I'll go. She just needs some sleep."

Gallie and I watch as the elevator door closes behind Alfie and Ria, and then we turn to each other. Gallie musters a weak smile which I return.

"You know—"

"So, they didn't probe her on kosonics," Gallie says.

"No, not yet. And something else I learned from Tommy is that Green is also heading up a koson weapons program."

"Big surprise, huh?" I'm not used to seeing Gallie sneer.

"You know, at this point, I'm wondering what it matters if Alfie reveals all to them: timeline transport, the whole damn thing. Is it a secret still worth keeping?"

Gallie is about to speak, pauses as if invalidating her first thought, and then says, "It's about trust. Do we want Green and his team to get new understanding? I can't predict how, but I know they'd abuse it."

"Knowing it's possible that they're not actually annihilating anyone might dampen their enthusiasm."

"What do they care? They're getting rid of inconvenient people either way. And it feels to me like educating Green just puts more tools at his disposal."

We sip the wine and grimace together.

"So what does come next? For us?" Gallie asks.

"For you and me?"

"And Alfie and Ria."

My planning to this point had had a twenty-four-hour horizon. I shrug. "At least you and I won't still be around when the world hits the wall."

"But everything will turn to absolute hell long before then. We're barely clinging on to civilization even now. When the world finds out—"

"We get out of here, I guess."

"To where?"

"Little point in heading to a different timeline. Every one of them will hit the wall, or at least that's the Bells' prediction."

"Agreed," Gallie says. "So taking Green's lead and jumping back is the obvious option, isn't it?"

I raise my eyebrows. "Go with them to Tomatotown?"

"Hell no," Gallie says, shaking her head vigorously. "We've got our own options, don't we? You're Joad Bevan, the intrepid time adventurer, after all. You must have friends everywhere and everywhen. Maybe you even have secret families out there?"

I grin. "You know I don't have that kind of energy."

"True. Just thought I'd ask." She places a hand on mine and pinches the back of it. "But we do have options, Joad."

I put my other hand on top of hers and squeeze it. "That's not what you want to do, Gallie—jump up the timeline."

No? she motions.

"What you want to do is get to the koson singularity to find…"

"To find Joad?" Her smile fades. "You know, the singularity might not even be a place… not an environment with spatial dimensions and—"

"Ria says she thinks it is, and Alfie agrees."

Gallie shakes her head. "We'd take that risk based on Ria's theory alone?" She smiles because she knows the answer.

"Trouble is, now all we have is just one depleted wrist accelerator between us. We're going to have to get our hands on some tackychemicals if we want to widen our options."

42

My mother and I were the discoverers of the koson particle, sibling of the tachyon. The practical implications of our findings needed to be explored, and we sought the help of Dr. Joad Bevan, formerly a senior figure in the TMA—quite the practical sort and, you might say, a time adventurer. It was many years after our seminal work on kosonics, and long after my mother's passing, that I had had something of a breakthrough in understanding the tachyon wall. My mother had set me in the right direction, but it had then taken quite a while to develop. I uncovered a holographic principle that allowed me to infer what is beyond the wall by studying the behavior of koson radiation near the wall's surface. But my excitement at the scientific discovery was brief and quickly dampened by the stark realization of its consequences.

Here are the salient points of my work as I understood it at the time. I concluded that there is a transition occurring in space and time. You can think of it as a wave traveling through space at the speed of light, so it cannot be seen coming except through hints offered by the behavior of tachyons and kosons at the wall. Ahead of the wavefront are the four dimensions of Einstein—three of space, one of time. (I will return to the limited adequacy of this four-dimensional picture presently.) In the wake of the wave is something quite different. There, the fourth dimension has made a critical transition. It has become a fourth spatial dimension, no different from the other three. Gone are the distinctive properties of time as a dimension, and behind the wall is a timeless universe. A spatial block—a cosmos that has more the attributes of a painting than a play. But it's a painting that cannot be admired because consciousness itself is linked inextricably to time and its passage. Each requires the other. On the far side of the wall, there is neither. The human experience—in fact any form of sentience—stops at the wall because the space beyond is not equipped to support it. And that wave happens to hit our little patch of the cosmos in the year 2088. It is manifested as the wall and is, literally, the end of time. No wonder then that tachyons, and their miraculous ability to sweep matter along the timeline, run into a dead end. My analysis led me to this conclusion and it is what I believed at that time.

Memoirs of Alfreda O. Bell
Personal Calendar: 79 years, 63 days

43
Joad

By the fourth sharp rap on our door I'm on my feet, peering through the peephole. *What the...* Alfie's face appears rounded in the lens, Ria behind her. I open the door, and Alfie sweeps past me as Ria shrugs an apology.

"I'm going," Alfie says, not to anyone in particular. "There's no way I go back to that place tomorrow."

"What time is it?" Gallie asks, squinting in the light from the corridor.

"Wait, wait." I close the door, turn on music, and gesture that we should sit around the coffee table.

We lean forward. "I can't do it," Alfie says, now speaking in a loud whisper. "This place is painful to me. Why would I help DTS? Why? And even if I wanted to I couldn't, not without my mother."

Gallie places a hand on Alfie's forearm. "Take a breath, Alfie."

"You're telling me how to breathe now? I don't want to take a fucking breath." Gallie squeezes her arm, possibly with affection but more likely to remind her that we are supposed to be whispering. "And it's just a matter of time before they start the interrogation on kosonics. They don't really give a shit about the tachyon wall. They're all going to evacuate anyway—leave behind the poor bastards not on their list."

"Okay, okay, Alfie," I say. "So what do you want to do?"

"Just get out of here, and right now."

"How?"

"How?" She glares at me. "What the hell do you think you're for, Joad? You're the one who's supposed to know how to get us out of tricky situations. Why do you think you're here?" She's beginning to break out of her whisper again and we all wave her to keep it down.

I look at Gallie who is barely suppressing a smile. "Then we need accelerators," I say. "Unless you think more conventional transport is practical. We'd need to find a car, maybe a working fuel station, then we could drive off through the dumpster fire that is Washington, DC."

"I can get us accelerators," Alfie says.

"From DTS?"

"Hell no. The people I met wouldn't be trusted with real hardware. I can get them from Mo. He's going to have accelerators."

"Would he be willing—"

"He'll do what I tell him."

"And how do you contact him?" I ask. "There'll be a tap on your phone, on all of our phones."

She points at my wrist accelerator.

"It's bone dry," I say.

"It's for communication too. At least across simultaneous time. For that it doesn't need the tackychemicals."

I look at the device on my wrist with admiration as I remove it and hand it to Alfie. "Okay, before you do that, let's figure out what the hell the plan is."

"Yeah, you never stuck me as much of a planner," Alfie says. For someone who has known me for so little time, I'm impressed by that insight.

"Well, now's the ideal time to start, I'd say."

"Do we need a full plan now?" Ria asks. "Let's just get out of here and then plan at our leisure."

"Makes sense," Gallie says. "But how does Mo get the accelerators to us? We're inside a tachyon shield."

"We meet him outside," I say.

"And how do we escape this prison?" Ria asks. "There are as many guards as residents."

Under the scrutiny of numerous security personnel, I glance behind me to make sure Gallie and the Bells are still in tow as we cross the hotel lobby. I'm about to reach for the brass bar of the hotel's main door when a guard inserts himself in front of me.

"What are you doing, sir?" He's affecting a politeness not intended to convince.

"We're going to a meeting at DTS," I say.

"This early? Where's your car?" He looks at the others behind me.

"We're going to get some air—walk there."

He smirks. "Oh, no. You don't want to do that, sir. It's not safe. Wait for your car."

I give him a *how dare you?* glare, but when it's clear that it is having no effect, I turn away and motion my team to follow. Plan A was never going to work.

Plan B seemed even less likely to pan out, but it was Gallie's idea, so dismissing it would be unwise and at odds with all experience. As we enter the kitchen, the staff prepping for breakfast look up, but their interest in us is short-lived. We wend through gleaming metal counters, industrial-scale appliances, and past pots and pans hanging from racks. Gallie asks a young, rosy-cheeked man in chef's whites where we'd find the delivery door, and after a pause to absorb the question, he points. We walk in single file, nodding as if familiar with some of the kitchen staff, until we arrive at the head of a corridor that turns off from the main kitchen work area. At the end of it is a wide rollup door, next to which a guard is sitting, a rifle in his lap. He is jolted from his repose and stands up to face us.

"They stole from me," Gallie cries out. Ria and I exchange an incredulous glance. The seemingly sincere hysteria in the timbre of Gallie's voice had shocked us—a tone and pitch I'd never heard from her before. She had told me there were people who called their DTS director a crazy old woman, and that she would draw on that.

"You can't be here," the guard says with practiced authority.

"But they stole—"

"Go back to your room. Call hotel security if something's been stolen."

"So what are you?" As the pitch of Gallie's voice rises even further, we step back around the corner to give her and the guard some privacy. "Why are you just standing there? Do something! They stole from me." She points toward the kitchen and I hear the guard's footsteps approaching. As the cast-iron skillet meets his skull, I feel the impact up to my elbow and drop the pan, shaking off the pain. The kitchen staff have suspended their preparations to take in the show, and with fingertips from brow, I give them an adios and follow the others down the delivery corridor. Ria and Alfie unlatch and lift the roller door and we duck under it onto the docking platform, then lower ourselves to the ground.

It's still dark outside and the streets are deserted, too early for office workers, too late for anarchists. We make our way briskly to the DC mall, panting vapor into the frigid morning air. The Capitol and the mall monuments had long since been in darkness to avoid unwanted attention. Alfie stops to confirm the coordinates I had given her for Mo, then after a brief journey, we circumnavigate the Smithsonian Museum Castle and enter the garden behind it.

Shit! There's a huddle of people at the center of the garden, their attention on something or someone in their midst. That's unlucky, although Alfie's searing glare gives me the impression that it has more to do with my bad planning than bad luck. We approach them slowly but their attention remains on whatever or whoever is at the center.

"That's Mo," Alfie says, walking ahead without curiosity as to whether we are following her. Mo Khara is at the center of the huddle holding what looks like a cardboard box. Alfie calls Mo's name, and I instantly wish I hadn't lost the argument about whether I should bring the guard's rifle. The group, who all seem to be men, turn to watch this assertive woman approaching them, the rest of us following close behind.

"You have them?" she calls out to Mo, without acknowledging the men who are now grinning at each other. Mo nods hesitantly.

"Who the fuck are you?" a gangly member of the pack asks, a look of casual violence in his eyes.

"Fuck off," Alfie says, reaching for the box.

"What's in the box?" he asks.

"What's in it is mine," Alfie replies without looking at him.

"No, no," he says, pushing Alfie aside. I pick up the pace to stand beside her.

"There's nothing that'd interest you," I say, the prospect of this ending matters not crossing my mind. Alfie places the box on the ground, opens the loose flaps, and takes out an accelerator, waving it in the thug's face.

"Electronics," she says. "Does nothing you'd be smart enough to understand."

The leader looks at his cohort, affecting a grin meant to assure them he's taking all of this in his stride. Meanwhile, Alfie places the accelerator on her wrist and taps in data. "Get yours," she says to me, but before I can react, I receive a sharp shove from behind and struggle to maintain my balance.

Then I hear *"Back off"* being shouted from a distance, and turn to see half a dozen silhouettes in the morning twilight, looking as though they may be pointing handguns in our direction. From behind them emerges another figure.

I had just recognized the absurd gunslinger gait of Athol Green when the first shot rang out from behind me. Some of the men surrounding Mo are now pointing their own pistols back at Green. Then the gunfire takes off.

"Down!" I shout, falling to my stomach as a barrage of bullets whip by above me. I carefully raise my head to look for Gallie, but don't initially see her. The gun battle comes to a quick end, and I sit up to see the surviving pack members running into the morning mist, leaving behind the motionless bodies of the fallen. I bound towards Gallie and Ria who are lying flat on the ground—neither is moving. My stomach dissolves into dread as I bend over Gallie. Her eyes are closed and I throw myself to my knees, cupping her muddied cheek. When I say her name, her eyes flutter open and she smiles up at me. With a delayed rush of adrenaline my heart begins to pound against my ribs as I help her sit up slowly. We look toward Ria who is still. Then I see it: the growing pool of blood beneath her head. Athol Green is looking down at me.

"You idiot," I say.

"Not what I wanted," he replies. "Why did you do this? We had a deal."

Alfie! I jump up and lope towards the fallen thugs, scanning around me frantically. I don't see her. Then I notice Mo, still standing and nursing a bloodied arm.

"Alfie?"

"She got away," he says.

"To where?"

He shakes his head.

44
Alt-Joad

I look over my shoulder to see Kora shrinking from colossus to human. Once we'd stepped into the shrink zone, I assumed we'd find ourselves in a community of some kind, but instead we're standing in a wooded area similar to the one I had traveled through when I first arrived on this absurd world. Is Nef like a set of Russian dolls—worlds within worlds where I'll be subjected to one spatial shrinkage after another?

I notice that Kora is nocking her bow with an arrow.

"What's wrong?"

"Listen."

Then I hear it too: the rustling of vegetation. Kora swings her bow, aiming at something behind me, and I turn, unslinging my rifle, then find the same target.

The man is the image of a Neanderthal: squat and stocky with a large nose, prominent brow ridges, and shallow forehead. But this Neanderthal is wearing a bright red jacket that reaches down to the knees of his short legs, with matching trousers and black leather boots. At first he's shocked, but then a smile creases his entire face.

"I'll need your help," he says in a loud and unexpectedly high-pitched voice. We lower our weapons, and after a moment, I realize he is waiting for a response.

"Okay," I say, and I look at Kora who is grinning at me.

"Thank you. I heard you speaking English and I'd like to know if I'm understandable. I suppose I must be. You see, I'm expected to have a command of the English language as it has been spoken over quite a tract of time; and as you know, it has evolved substantially, so I had to make a guess."

I nod, mesmerized by the incongruity of it all. Perhaps he isn't what he looks like and is just a guy with unique features. Yet, I have briefly crossed paths with a few Neanderthals in my travels and I'm now recalling that the high-pitched voice was one of their surprising characteristics—although this vocabulary is broader than I'd remembered. "Your language is very understandable," I say. Kora is sniggering behind me, and I cast her a reproving glance, although from the escalation of her reaction to the man, she may not be familiar with that look. The Neanderthal smiles even wider, as if sharing Kora's joke.

"Thank you," he says to me. "My name is James." I avoid Kora's eyes. "May I ask, why are you here?" This question might have seemed threatening from anyone else.

"The palace," I reply, looking around us but seeing only trees and undergrowth. "We're looking for it."

"Of course, yes. Would you like me to take you to it?"

"That'd be… yes, please."

With this he turns and walks off. After a few steps he looks back, and I realize we are supposed to follow. It takes only a few minutes to emerge from the forest to the sight of… it's a palace. That would not be a fanciful description of the structure that's standing about half a mile away. In fact, it looks like an absurd stereotype of a palace, as if taken from a book of fairy tales.

It is a pale structure, perhaps of sandstone or even marble, with all the features you'd expect from a fairy tale: towers, spires, turrets, and gables. I can't help but smile. The closest to this I had seen was a castle commissioned by King Ludwig II of Bavaria—a ludicrously fanciful structure—but compared to this, it was an office block. As I'm trying to formulate a reasonable question, James the Neanderthal has already begun to pose his own.

"How long do you think it'd take us to walk directly to the palace?"

I'm nonplussed by the question and shrug. "I, er... a few minutes?"

This reply pleases him. "Actually no. The direct route would take us through some regions of severe spatial dilation. It'd take us three days."

He waits for our astonishment, so I dutifully raise my eyebrows. The truth is that my threshold for surprises has become astronomically high over the past few days.

"But don't worry, we have another path."

We seem to be in a shallow valley at the far end of which is the palace. He points up the valley slope.

"Who built the palace?" I ask as we begin to climb.

He looks back down at us. "The Team," he says, seemingly confused by the banality of my question.

I glance at Kora to see if that answer makes any sense to her, but there is no sign that it had. I continue with my line of questioning. "Who's the Team? And why did they build a palace?"

"It's what they wanted," comes the reply. "They made a lot of careful decisions, so I think the palace design would have been one of them."

"What kind of decisions, James?"

"Oh, well..."

I have the sense that there are so many examples that he's having difficulty picking one.

He continues after a moment. "Which species to import, like the best arable crops based on factors like food production capability, yield stability, nitrogen efficiency, biodiversity—that sort of thing. That's my field so I know something about it. But they went through the same process with animal importation—you know, feed-to-food conversion, terrain adaptability, environmental impact, a mix of protein chiralities, etcetera. And safety to humans, of course. I must add," he says, chuckling, "a few unintended species got through the net, but that was inevitable."

This is a Neanderthal? "And these species were selected from up and down the timeline?" I ask.

"Yes, of course. Ninety-nine percent of species had gone for good before the end, and they didn't want to restrict themselves. They wanted an optimal mix."

"The end? Of—"

"Nearly there," he says.

We crest the hill and on the far side is a vast expanse of a golden crop, the breeze making waves on its surface.

"Barley?"

"For malt. Most of the crops we have meet the sort of criteria I mentioned, but some were brought here out of love." He grins as if I should know what that means. Then we set out along the ridge that leads to the palace.

I'm beginning to notice that the field has speckles of something dark, and that they are moving. A voice calls out, high-pitched and raspy, to which James replies, but I understand none of it. At first, I take the person stepping out from the crops to be a child, but then I see the wide, flat nose and receding forehead. Most distinctively of all, he's very short and slight—less than four feet tall—and wearing a loose linen shirt and trousers. Kora giggles at the sight, and the small person shoots her a look that indicates he is perhaps less magnanimous than James. Our escort doesn't stop so we keep following him.

"It's mainly Flores who do the harvesting," James says, anticipating my question. "The human species the Team imported were mainly those with the wherewithal to organize and contribute: Denisovans, Flores, me." He simpers. "But mainly Homo sapiens, of course."

I decide to take this information in my stride, at least until I can pose a few intelligent questions. As we continue on, Kora is still turning periodically to gape at the Flores, who are now looking back indignantly. Then she passes me to walk by James's side, and they begin to exchange words I can't make out.

45

The problem with senility, or with losing one's mind in general, is that the faculties required to notice it can be precisely those that are being lost. And bear in mind that physics senility arrives much earlier than the cognitive kind. This has happened to many once-prominent scientists that it would be indelicate to list. But I flatter myself that my mind was still perfectly intact when, several years after gaining an understanding of the wall, I had some additional insights. I reminded myself that if one were to reject an idea purely on the grounds that it seems utterly ludicrous, then my mother and I would never have pursued koson theory. Nor, for that matter, would the world have been given relativity, quantum mechanics, and other theories that had violated an everyday sense of reality.

Let me begin by observing that many had wondered why we inhabit a universe with three dimensions of space and yet only one of time. To some, this had always seemed like an unequitable arrangement. But then, an additional time dimension was discovered and this had seemed to help redress the balance. Tau time was uncovered first, but then yet another time dimension revealed itself. So then we arrived at three of space and three of time, which seemed satisfying. But the additional two dimensions of time were rather feeble and inert. We understood that only conventional time (as we call it) is physically coupled to the human

TIME WALL

experience—to consciousness and all the other symptoms of passing time. It took a while for us to understand that, in fact, consciousness couples to all three of the time dimensions, but the coupling with conventional time is overwhelmingly strong, making the additional two time dimensions entirely unnoticeable in the course of human experience. That all made sense to the scientific community—at least what was left of it.

But here is the breakthrough of which I am quite proud. It occurred to me that parallel timelines could, in principle, experience differing degrees of coupling between consciousness and the three time dimensions. So I could envision a timeline in which the dominant cause of consciousness and experience is not conventional time, but one of the other two varieties. As I pondered this notion, its implications began to crystallize. My thought was this: What happens at the tachyon wall is that conventional time transitions into just another spatial dimension—an event that portends a compelling and definitive finale for us all. But my analysis showed that there existed no such wall for the other time dimensions. So a world in which consciousness is strongly coupled to another of those time dimensions might be entirely untouched by the cosmic catastrophe. I realized that in that world life might go on, although I posited that spacetime behavior in such a strange timeline might be rather perverse by our familiar standards. And then I remembered some work done by one Ria Bell (a relation, of sorts) who predicted the likely existence of a koson singularity that might take the form of a timeline. It was then that I began to connect some intriguing dots.

Memoirs of Alfreda O. Bell
Personal Calendar: 79 years, 87 days

46
Joad

A torrent of water has passed under the bridge since Athol Green fired me in this office. Gallie is sitting beside me and Green is stationed behind his desk in his elevated seat. I touch Gallie's arm and it's cold. I want to offer words of comfort but I'll wait until we're alone, although I can't yet imagine what those words will be. She withdraws her arm and places it in her lap.

"Seems I'm making a career out of saving your ass, Joad." Green smirks and waits for a response but gets none. "I just don't understand you."

"Whose bullet killed our friend?" I say. "One of yours?"

He shrugs. "What does it matter now? You'd all be dead if we hadn't taken action."

"You take a lot of action, don't you, Athol?" Gallie says, and he smiles at her.

"Very unfortunate about your friend. I'm sorry for your loss." Then he turns back to me. "You knew how important Alfreda Bell is to us. Why would you do this?"

"Important to making a better weapon?" My response is impulsive but now it's out.

He affects weariness. "Weapon? Not again, Joad. The wall is my concern. My only concern."

"Escaping the wall is your concern, as are kosonic weapons."

"This is getting—"

"Athol. I know about the Ark Project, and I know about the weapons program you're heading."

His smile fades and he begins to tap his desk. "Where are you getting this from?"

"A reliable source, as they say. Very reliable."

He stands and sits on the edge of his desk, facing us. "Where did the Bell woman go?"

"I don't know. She's very independent." He stares at me, as if looking for some sign in my face. "I'm curious, who qualifies to be part of the Ark Project? And how do you pick which populations to destroy? Do you confer with the foreign entities who are doing the same thing to their people? Coordinate? Or do you just pick victims who are a domestic inconvenience?"

Green rolls his eyes as if dealing with an ill-informed child. "You may have noticed there's chaos out there. Some of us are charged with the responsibility of dealing with it."

"But, you see, Athol, you're not vanishing rioters and anarchists, are you. I think there are too many of them and they have friends, sympathizers, and families. Not good politics to kill them. So here's my theory: What you're doing is making sure foreign states are aware we have a capability, in case they see opportunity to take advantage. A sort of deterrent, where you annihilate communities, but only ones that won't be missed."

Green throws his head back and grins.

"Like I said, it's just a theory," I say. "And understand, I'm not accusing you personally. This comes from higher up, right? So someone is going to be exceedingly disappointed that you lost Alfreda Bell—your unique asset."

"You're quite clever, Joad. I'd never really seen that in you before."

"And you're quite the moron. That I have always seen. And by the way, the woman shot dead out there—she was also a founding expert in kosonics. So you lost yourself two invaluable assets this morning. And you killed one of them. I think your bosses will take a serious interest in that. No?"

"Bullshit," he says, his lips curled into a savage smile. He turns to Gallie and surveys her for a moment. "And might you be yet another expert?"

"God, no," Gallie replies, raising her palms in protest.

He ponders for a moment and then jumps to his feet. "Come on. I'm going to take you somewhere."

As we exit his office, a large minder with a ginger crew cut, bulging neck, and a suit a size too small joins us. There's no conversation as we descend to the basement, taking a turn along a corridor I don't recognize. We reach a sturdy door and Green applies his pass to the keypad, then jabs in a code. There's a resonant *clunk* and Green pushes the door open. The first thing I notice inside are the racks of bottles and cylinders lining the wall. Ahead of us is what could only be a bulk acceleration cylinder, although nothing like as large as the one in Risley—maybe ten feet in diameter. The room is cold and brightly lit, and a ventilation fan is laboring above us.

Gallie leans in to me. "This room doesn't exist in my DTS. Anyone trusted with tackychemicals was in Risley."

Green beckons us to catch up and then dons a wrist accelerator that had been lying on a table, handing another to his guard. The design is familiar, with a screen and keypad on the wrist and the chemical chambers extending up the forearm. They look very cumbersome to me, having become accustomed to the sleek, little devices Mo Khara had designed.

"No accelerators for us?" I ask.

Green just smiles and opens a cupboard, removing from it something that looks like a flare gun painted white.

"You'll find this interesting." He breaks the gun like an old-fashioned revolver, and from its chamber removes the single slug, which he holds up between forefinger and thumb to show us. The bullet is cylindrical, rounded at one end, about an inch across and twice as long. "Can you guess what this is?" he asks, but doesn't wait for a reply. "This contains three compartments—one per tackychemical. When it strikes its target, the compartment boundaries shatter and the chemicals mix."

"Giving you a blast of…?"

"Of kosons—a heavy dose."

"And your victim vanishes," I say. "A little crude, don't you think?"

"Very crude, Joad," he says, reloading the weapon and tucking it into the back of his belt. "That's why we need Dr. Bell—to bring a little sophistication to our technology. Her man Khara knows the broad mechanics of producing measured koson fluxes, but it's the science and the motivations we need to understand. Anyway," he says, pressing a pad on the acceleration cylinder that causes its door to rotate open. "Get in."

"Where are we going?" I ask.

"We're going to the wall."

47
Alt-Joad

The scale and architectural detail of the edifice before us is coming into focus. The palace gables are decorated with reliefs of figures representing times and places, although with no apparent logic—a Roman patrician conversing with a cowboy, an Egyptian queen offering a cup of something to a kid in shorts and sneakers. There are balconies with stone balustrades at multiple levels, some occupied by people whose attention we have now garnered. James points at someone on one of the balconies for Kora's benefit and waves. Then he turns to me and suggests we leave our weapons here. Even in the unlikely scenario that these people are unfriendly, we would be seriously outnumbered, so I throw my rifle to the ground and Kora places her bow and quiver on top of it.

We pass through a wide porte cochère into a courtyard containing maybe two dozen long wooden tables around which people are enjoying what looks like jugs of beer. Many are wearing loose floral shirts and colorful trousers, and some have streaks of bright color in their hair and beards. I stop, taking in the bizarre scene around me, and then have to jog to catch up with James and Kora. They're starting up a staircase that leads to the interior of the structure.

Now we're in a grand hall with enormous crystal chandeliers high above. A marble staircase leads to a mezzanine with a mosaic-tiled floor and walls covered in LED screens displaying moving images. People are walking in every direction, entering, exiting, ascending, descending, all while expertly navigating one another, making it feel like a busy train station.

I stand, gaping around me, waiting for any kind of mental model of what this place might be. Nothing useful occurs to me. I turn to express my bewilderment to Kora and James, but they're gone. I scan the hall and mezzanine, but spotting them in the throng would be unlikely.

I feel like a lost child in a department store. Lots of languages are being spoken, some sounding archaic, and I'm not sure who to approach. I insert myself into the human flow ascending the grand staircase to the mezzanine, keeping pace and trying to appear at home. The traffic gradually thins out as people turn off into high-ceilinged corridors, marble staircases, and arched doors. What eventually comes into view ahead of me is comfortingly modern. It's a metallic door, the sort that is bound to require a credential to open. I watch as the door swings open for the woman walking ahead of me, but she didn't seem to present a pass of any kind. I assume she must have been carrying a transponder chip. The door closes behind her, and I slow down to avoid slamming into it. And then it opens again—seemingly for me—so I quickly step through as if it would realize its error.

I enter onto a platform with a sunken space in front of me that is maybe the area of a football field. It looks like a vast office space containing work cubicles with walls of glass. There are people inside the cubicles and shifting images are being projected onto the glass walls—some looking like data tables and graphs, others like landscapes and buildings. Someone brushes past me to exit and I apologize distractedly. Indistinct chatter fills the huge room and as I look up, I see clouds drifting past the high, tinted glass ceiling. Suddenly I notice someone at the foot of the platform steps watching me. A dark-skinned woman with a shaved head and a streak of pink painted on her pate. She says something to me in a contralto voice, but I don't understand.

"I'm sorry," I say, "did not get that."

She pauses as if to analyze what she has heard. "Late English. Are you a visitor?"

I nod. "Yes, a visitor."

"From which community?" Someone behind her laughs loudly and she looks away for a moment.

"I'm not from a community."

She smiles at me. "You arrived on Nef alone?"

"I did."

"A singleton! I'll take you to our singleton desk." She beckons me to follow. We navigate a tortuous path between the glass cubicles. I try to read some of the graphs and charts as we pass, but none of it is intelligible. We soon arrive at a cubicle that contains a rotund, heavily-spectacled man with a pug nose and wild gray hair around his ears but little of it on top.

"A singleton visiting," she says and promptly walks off.

"Not a good day for it," he says, sounding harassed, and then looks up at me. "Okay, okay. You arrived recently?" His English is heavily accented although I cannot place it. "You understand that even if your arrival seems recent to you, to me it was quite a while ago." There's a flash of light, as if my photograph has been taken, and then he taps his fingers against one of the cubicle walls, causing the display of a data stream followed by an image. "That's you." Before the image vanishes I see myself lying in the vegetation patch that had been my landing site.

"Yes. What is all of this?"

He stares at me as he interprets the question. "Well, it's the singleton desk."

"This whole place, I mean."

"This? You mean the Light Hub? It's where we track arrivals. Is that what you're asking?"

"Communities?"

"Yes, arrivals of communities mainly, although there can be smaller groupings—even singletons like you." He grins. "That's why I have a job."

"Arrivals across the whole—"

"Yes, across Nef, and from every timeline."

I decide that asking what he means by that would be a distraction from more imperative questions.

"It's here we make sure new arrivals are catered for—that a mentoring community finds them. Can be pretty terrifying when you just show up here. Well, you must know that."

"Who was my mentoring community?" I ask.

He furrows his brow and quickly turns away to scrutinize his wall. "A few get through the net—and not only singletons," he says, now sounding defensive. "If you knew how many people arrive here... It can be overwhelming." He begins prodding at the moving graphics. "Maybe we can talk again later. This is just one of those days, data reporting and all." He rotates his chair away from me, and it seems our conversation is over. "Seriously, now is a bad time," he says over his shoulder.

I stand still for a moment, being ignored by the singleton desk manager and without any sense of what comes next. Finding Kora and James seems like an impossible task, and I really have no place to be. Then I remember the beer garden, and a plan—a simple one—falls into place. I leave the cubicle to retrace my steps, and rejoin the human flow.

Stepping out into the courtyard, I join the heavy foot traffic getting bottlenecked at the porte cochère. Maybe this is what a change of shift looks like as workers return to their local communities while others arrive to start their day.

Some of the people who are on their way out are taking a detour to the beer garden, and the serving counter in front of the small structure that must be supplying the drinks is clogging up rapidly. A parapet sign, in bold blackletter font, reads *The Merry Crab* and above it is an image of a crab flailing its claws and eyestalks. As I approach the bar, I feel a jab to my leg and turn to see Kora and James grinning up at me from their table.

"Where the hell did you go?" I ask as I sit down. James says he'll get me a beer and leaves Kora to deal with me. She watches him walk away and then returns her attention to me, still smiling.

"Where did you disappear to?" she asks. "You were there one minute and then… gone." My highly peeved expression does not register with her. "It's amazing here, isn't it?"

"Is it? You're not eager to get back to Underbridge?"

"No." Her expression conveys the stupidity of my question.

"Where did you go to after I got lost?"

"James was showing me around. All the things they have here…"

These are among the longest sentences I have heard from Kora, each one a soliloquy by her standards. She looks around excitedly, glancing often at the bar to see if James is returning.

When he gets back he places a tall jar of beer in front of me, which I sip. *Oh!* I nod in approval.

"I'm sorry we were split up," James says in his powerful, high-pitched voice. Kora is grinning, so I follow her stare to a nearby table of Flores. She points at them and I grab her finger, pulling it down.

"I visited the Light Hub," I say.

"Really?" James replies. "It must have interested you greatly. I don't know much about it—not my job." He takes a deep draft of his beer that nearly empties a full jar. "Would you like me to arrange sleeping accommodations for you?"

"Yes, we'd appreciate that," I say.

"No," Kora quickly interjects. "Just you. I'm staying with James in his village." I didn't know what a look of embarrassment would look like for a Neanderthal, but now I may.

"Is it a Neanderthal village?" I ask.

He shakes his head and I sense that I may have offended him, but the wide, warm smile is not at bay for long. "Would you prefer to stay in the palace?"

"Yes, thank you, James," I reply, then take another swig. Without having known, it's exactly what this singleton needs.

48

In making our sanctuary, we had all the resources of the past available to us. But to claim it as our creation would be an exaggeration, I suppose, because as Ria Bell had speculated, the singularity was indeed a place with spatial extension and time and matter. In fact, it was far more than that—it had its own diversity of life, albeit entirely vegetation with little food value. Yet the perverse nature of its spacetime metric, in which we sometimes couldn't take a hundred paces without experiencing a temporal or spatial dilation, made it abundantly clear that this was not a timeline like any other.

My team was the best I could assemble. It would have amused those who knew me in my formative years to learn that I had not only become part of a team, but had formed it. Me, Alfreda Bell, the hermit researcher (but for my mam) who believed that any team was bound to take on the characteristics of its dumbest member, had undergone this sea change of attitude. You see, I had begun to understand how a team can work. I understood that even though the others might not equal me in their physical insight, they can nevertheless bring other valuable attributes to the team such as practical wisdom, hands-on know-how, courage, strength, and even empathy and compassion had their roles. This I first learned from a small band of people that I came to trust, and, as I later realized, maybe even love. But that was long before the sanctuary project, and now I needed a much larger team, a team that could help me create a world—the place we came to call Nef. It was on my journeys up, down, and across timelines that I learned of a group who called themselves Allfours—illicit and mischievous time travelers who had become the bane of TMA's existence. This made them my kind of people. And they had practical assets: bulk accelerators that could be adapted for koson transport, seemingly endless supplies of the tackychemicals we needed, and an expansive cross-temporal knowledge of technological, agricultural, and infrastructural resources. And as a bonus, almost everyone in this close-knit group was impressively bright, one particularly sharp fellow called Casy even claiming to be the son of the great adventurer Joad Bevan.

It turns out that an issue we never needed to confront was the logistical challenge involved in the wholesale shunting of populations from their doomed timelines. That work was being done for us by seedy powers who mistakenly thought they were annihilating their unwanted people; whereas, in fact, their crude weapons were simply sending their victims to the singularity—to Nef. And these populations were quite large, more than enough for us to cope with. So it seems that, in the end, the meek did indeed inherit the earth.

And if, by some quirk of nature in a universe that none of us fully understands, my mother were to see Nef, I would ask her, "Hey Mam, is my palace whimsical enough for you?"

Memoirs of Alfreda O. Bell
Personal Calendar: 79 years, 210 days

49
Joad

We step out of the acceleration cylinder into the same room, although now the chemical racks are gone, the floor is covered with lab detritus, and it's even colder than it had been before. The fortified door is still there and we exit through it. We're met by a smell of rust and damp. The corridor is illuminated by only a few flickering lights, and items of trashed office furniture are stacked up against the walls. Following Green through this dilapidated DTS, we finally step out of the stairwell into the lobby. I'm watching Gallie's reaction to this place, and she does not seem to be taking it well. Even though this had never been her DTS, the surrounding decay is something that had happened to an organization that had been part of her life. Half the lobby windows are spider-webbed with cracks, some with a bullet hole at their center. There's a smell of urine, but also of something worse—maybe a decomposing body, although there's no visible sign of it.

"Not pretty, is it?" Green says, glancing back. "The air's better outside." He leads us out to the atrium, and we descend the few steps to the sidewalk. Dark, heavy clouds threaten rain, and I catch a flash of lightning in the distance.

There are no people around, only abandoned cars that had long ago run out of fuel, and looking down Independence Avenue I see the once grand and elegant buildings now covered in graffiti. Not a single window in the Smithsonian Museum Castle is intact, although the flags on its tower are still fluttering defiantly in the wind.

"Do we want to get too far away from the accelerator?" I ask.

"Are you nervous?" Green reaches into his pocket and takes out a small device, which he jabs.

"Five minutes and thirty-eight seconds," a woman's voice announces.

"Just a reminder," he says.

"Is that when we hit the wall?" Gallie asks.

"Exactly. So, might I convince you to tell me where we'd find Alfreda Bell? She is extremely important to us."

"We tell you what you want to know or else you leave us here? That it?" The guard who accompanied us through is nervously looking up at the clouds, as if the wall might be seen descending on us. "Look, Athol, I know we could tell you everything and you'd still leave us here. Right? We're in possession of too much embarrassing information about you."

Green snorts. "Oh yes. With all your credibility you'd definitely be believed. A man I had to fire who is now a teacher in that fine ivy league in southern Iowa."

"Okay. But you know what? I'm tired," I say. "I'm so fucking tired. A life of chaos, absurd dangers, and now all of this. Can't remember when I last slept through the night. Right now, oblivion is sounding pretty restful to me."

Four minutes exactly.

"I understand that," Athol says, only now seeming to notice the desolate landscape in front of us. "We picked quite a career for ourselves, didn't we? Quite an era to be born into for that matter. But tell me, Joad, how would you have liked your life to be different?"

"I wish I'd met fewer people."

Green chuckles and sits on the low wall that borders the DTS atrium.

"I know the picture you have of me. You're the great Joad Bevan, savior of histories, defender of the timeline, and protector of all that is good." He looks up at the flags flying above the castle. "But I'm trying to do a little good myself. To control the chaos, to understand our fate. Why would you want to stand in the way of that?"

"Here's an interesting fact for you, Athol," Gallie says. "In a different timeline I'm your boss."

He arches his brows. "I don't think so."

"Oh, it's true," I say.

"Really? Well, how about that. You see, I'm not a tusker. We senior DTS staff are given a choice and I figured, why add that extra anguish to my life? I'll just live the timeline I'm given."

"I didn't say I *was* your boss in a different timeline. I said I *am* your boss in a different timeline."

"And what exactly does that mean, good lady?"

"Good lady? Well, it means I'm the secretary of the DTS... in that timeline."

"This doesn't seem to me like the right time to be wasting it."

Two minutes exactly.

"It's the truth. I have my own version of you. And I'm afraid he's not that different."

"Sir." The guard clears his throat. "We're getting close."

"Nervous?" Green smiles at his subordinate. "Then go."

"Sir, it's just that—"

"Go!" Green gives his guard a dismissive wave, and I turn in time to see the minder vanish, feeling the faint movement of air typical of a close acceleration event.

"Can you imagine having a security professional like that in TMA?" Green shakes his head. "I've been dealt a very poor hand."

One minute exactly.

"The fact is," Gallie says, "you know almost nothing about kosonics—about its real significance."

Green looks at me as if for confirmation that he should bother listening to Gallie, and then turns to her. "Then tell me all about it. What is its significance?"

"Sure, but not here. We're going to need more than one minute." She begins up the steps towards the DTS entrance.

"No, no, no. Is your Athol Green a moron?"

Forty seconds.

Green taps his wrist accelerator. "I'm about to leave you now, but look on the bright side. Maybe the wall is not what we think. Maybe it'll just come and go, and the world will go on. Perhaps we're all getting worked up about a tempest in a tea cup and it'll be one big non-event."

Twenty-five seconds.

"Why don't you wait with us and see," I ask, looking up into the sky as if to see a harbinger of what is to come, but there's only a silent flash of lightning—the sign of a storm that will never have the chance to arrive.

Twenty seconds.

I follow Gallie up the atrium steps, but we don't have nearly enough time to get away. Then I stop to look down on Green hunched over his accelerator screen. It's a leap I could have taken with impunity in my younger years, and now with nothing to lose, it's a riskless option for different reasons. I do it, landing behind Green, and deliver a sharp blow to his temple before the pain has a chance to shoot up from my ankles.

Ten seconds.

I ignore my agony.

Eight seconds.

My heart thumps as I roll him over and take the white pistol from his belt. Gallie is at the top of the steps, wide-eyed.

"Love you, Gallie," I call out to her, "in every timeline, every world." I raise the gun.

Three seconds.

She shakes her head, mouthing *No*.
I take aim at the step she's standing on…
Two seconds.
… and pull the trigger. There's a slight recoil, and then she's gone. I look back down at Green, whose eyes are open but unseeing.
One second.
I feel a spot of rain on my cheek and look into the sky. *Well, it's about ti—*

50
Alt-Joad

I'd had the quest of finding the palace, but now that has gone. It had given me focus, purpose, so I didn't fill my days torturing myself with memories of Gallie—of imagining the warmth of her body as I sit by her, of telling each other the same old jokes, of us falling asleep side by side.

Now, my only distraction is sitting at the singleton desk with my newfound friend, Hakob. I'm an irritation to him, no question, but I've leveraged his guilt at having mishandled my arrival on Nef. I'd watch singletons arrive on his wall screen, seeing them frozen as they appear. Hakob explained that this is because of the frenetic pace at which time is passing in the palace compared to most of Nef. Men, women, and children from across the globe flash before us, their faces sometimes contorted in anguish from whatever circumstances had put them in the crosshairs. Hakob's job is to simply apprise the closest community of their arrival.

Talking between the duties his job demanded, he introduced me to the science of kosonics, inter-timeline transportation, and koson singularity theory, most of which was incomprehensible to me, although I suspect this was partly because Hakob didn't really understand any of it himself. He did no better a job at explaining the violet shaft of light above the palace, but I now gather that it's part of the laser communication system that supports the massive data transfer needs of the Light Hub.

Sometimes I'd stroll the palatial halls, where I discovered lecture theaters, meeting rooms, dining areas, equipment warehouses, power centers, and computing complexes, among other things. Some had wall-mounted video screens that told the story of the woman who had founded the palace and made Nef habitable. I'd seen Kora only once since we'd arrived and that had been from a distance. She had been walking beside James with little space between them—laughing, but I suspect it was no longer at him.

After a week at the palace I'm sensing that my ability to leverage Hakob's guilt is reaching its limit. He has taken to telling me about the fascinating cultures in the surrounding communities that he's sure would interest me.

"I've got a lot of arrival activity right now, so I really can't talk today."

"That's fine," I say. He looks at me expectantly, but when I show no sign of leaving, he sighs and gets back to work. Images of arrivals flash up on his screen, and he's correct—the arrival rate does seem higher than normal. The usual mix of facial expressions flash across his screens—shocked, unsuspecting, terrified, even a few inexplicable grins.

"Stop!" I push Hakob aside to get closer to his screen. "Go back one." When he starts to protest, I repeat, "Back one, Hakob, c'mon." Muttering to himself, he brings up the image, and I stare at it. My heart races. "Yes, her."

He taps something into his wall. "She's close to a community, so no problem. Why do—"

"Where?" I ask. "Which community? I need to find her."

"Find her? What do you mean?" Hakob looks perplexed. "We've detected her and we'll have the assigned community recover her."

I rotate his seat so he's facing me. "I mean I need to get to her."

"Oh," he says, seemingly reconciled to the fact that posing further questions to the crazy visitor would be futile. "I can map you a route. Hold on." He turns to his window screen and taps onto it as I watch, although I can make nothing of the display. "So, optimal route, here to there…"

"Yes, c'mon." I'm trying to control my breathing.

"This is it," he says, pointing at data I can't interpret.

"How long will it take me to get there?"

"Depends on your pace and resting needs, of course, but I'd say… oh, twenty years."

I stand back. "Did you say…"

"Twenty-ish years."

"That's insane."

"Well, the problem is, you'd have to go through a lot of spatial shrink zones that can't be circumnavigated. They really bump up travel time. But if it helps, given her location and with time dilation, she'll only experience about six weeks over the duration of your journey." His smile is an earnest one. "The size of Nef is really a good thing. We have to accommodate a lot here."

"Twenty years is assuming I walk? Is there another mode of transportation?"

"Like what?"

"Can I accel there?"

Hakob's brow furrows as he digests my question. "You mean a tachyon accel? No, no. Of course not. There's no tachyonics on Nef—we don't tick on conventional time."

"Conventional time!" *Whatever the hell I'm being told is just too much to pursue.*

"Look, I'll give you the route, and then you decide," Hakob says, turning away, seemingly pleased he's found something that may get rid of me. "But I can't let you sit here anymore—these arrivals deserve my full attention." His tone conveys a determination that my interruptions have come to an end.

I try to picture Gallie's image—the one I had just seen. Her expression had been one of shock, but not of fear or of pain. *She's okay. I think she's okay.*

Kora, James, and I are standing outside the porte cochère. We hear laughter from the beer garden on the other side of the palace gate and we smile as if sharing their joke.

"Are you sure you want to do this?" Kora asks me, turning to James for his support. I pull her towards me and kiss her forehead, and then James hands me my rifle.

"Just in case," he says, lowering his usually powerful voice to a high-pitched whisper. "There are a few species that got in despite the Team."

I hold out my hand and he encases it gently in his thick fingers. Then I turn away from the palace and from my friends, and I begin to walk.

"Good luck," I hear Kora call out. "I like you too, Joad."

I raise my hand and wave but don't look back.

Gallie has only six weeks to wait. And I have only twenty years. But what the hell else have I to do? I smile to myself. We'll be near contemporaries again, just as we'd been when we first met a lifetime ago in a small town in eastern Washington state. All I have to do is live long enough and not get lost. I feel in my pocket for the navigation device Hakob had given me, take a deep breath, and pick up the pace.

51
Alt-Joad

They stand before me like colossal statues. But now that inspires in me no awe, no confusion. I know that as I exit the shrink zone my size will approach theirs, and as I begin to share their time rate, they'll accelerate into motion. They are children dressed in jeans and T-shirts, kicking a ball to each other—a ball that had been stuck in mid-flight but is now slowly beginning to fall. I look over the side of my small row boat at a reflection in the still water of a man with thin white hair and a beard. Yet, for many years I had not minded the lines that had etched themselves into my face, because I'd known that as each one appeared, I was closer to Gallie. But now, as I approach the bank, it seems to have been far too long to let myself hope.

I step out of the boat to wade the last few yards, pulling the craft behind me. The children have stopped their game and gathered around, watching me drag my boat onto the bank. They are saying something to me in what sounds like a Semitic language and I can only smile at them.

"Sorry, I don't understand." One of them grabs my hand and pulls me towards a path that rises from the riverbank. With my entourage of children I reach the ridge. They must be recent arrivals as most of the ramshackle structures of their sprawling community below look like they have come from Uffern, although I see a few new building projects that are making use of Nefish timber. With all the experiences I've had by now, I think I'll be able to help these people.

We must not yet be at our destination because the small child is still pulling on my hand, hopefully taking me to someone who speaks a language I can understand. Ahead is a group of half a dozen people seated on blankets, and their conversation stops as they see us approaching. The woman at their center turns to see what had gotten their attention.

I fall to my knees and try to look at her again, but my vision is blurred by tears. After a moment, I feel her kneel beside me, and she kisses my cheek. I grope for her hand and squeeze it.

And time, the thing that had been the bane of my life, is now all I want.

ACKNOWLEDGEMENTS

I thank my wife, Heather, and my sister, Julia, whose suggestions always make my books better. My son, Stephen, created the book cover. He and my other son, Gareth, are often in my head as I create my protagonists. Erika Steeves was my copyeditor and, as always, did a top-notch job.

ABOUT THE AUTHOR

S. D. Unwin started out as a theoretical physicist searching for the Holy Grail of a quantum theory of gravity. He later turned his mathematical skills to analyzing and communicating catastrophic risk, from nuclear mishaps to major earthquakes. He has now settled happily on writing science fiction. Hailing originally from Manchester in the United Kingdom, Bainbridge Island in Puget Sound is where he calls home.

SDUnwin.com

Follow on Facebook:
facebook.com/unwinbooks

Also by S. D. Unwin

The Magni

The One Second Per Second Time Travel Trilogy:

One Second Per Second
Fall Of Time
Time Wall

Printed in Dunstable, United Kingdom